I0547821

TOCABAGA 6

THE DIMACHAERUS CLAN

MISSING IN ACTION

THOMAS H. WARD

TOCABAGA 6:

THE DIMACHAERUS CLAN

MISSING IN ACTION

by

THOMAS H. WARD

ISBN-13: 978-0692336069

ISBN-10: 0692336060

Copyright © 2014. All rights reserved. No part of this publication may be reproduced, distributed, or transmitted in any form or by any means, including photocopying, recording, or other electronic mechanical methods.

This book is a work of fiction. Names, characters, and incidents are a product of the author's imagination or used fictitiously. Any resemblance to persons, living or dead is entirely coincidental.

Transcendent Publishing
www.transcendentpublishing.com

PREFACE

How did our country get this way? My thinking is it was a number of things but it was also an overzealous President who was pushing for more control of the government to make a truly socialist state.

The President started a draft, but not for the military, for the new Federal Police Force or FPF. Their job would be to start green safe zones in the cities and guard the electric power plants and water supplies. They were to keep things running normal and generally enforce the laws. The Federal Police have all the same weapons, trucks, and tanks that the Army does. There are now 50,000 new Policemen. Even this number cannot control the situation.

The President put into effect Presidential

Executive Order 13603 which declares that all property belongs to the Federal Government: your house, money, guns, and even your kids. They can tell you where to live and where to work.

The Military is split over whether to follow the President's orders and violate the US constitution or to support the people. The normal Army is standing down but the Special Forces which include the Army Rangers, Delta Force, Airborne troops, Navy Seals, and other special operations have taken the side of the people and the Constitution. It's a civil war over the rights' of the people versus the government.

Years before, things weren't making much sense especially when the government took control of the news media. It became state owned so the only news we received was what the Federal Government wanted us to hear. Back in 2013 the NSA started to tap our phones, read our emails, and Facebook pages. We were all being watched, we were all suspected of doing something wrong. We were having our Bill of Rights violated in the name of government security, and no one did anything about it.

Benjamin Franklin once said, "He who sacrifices freedom for security deserves neither."

Unemployment shot up to 55% and everyone knew that things were changing as more and more acts of violence were reported across the nation. Riots, robberies, shootings, explosions, and even attacks on police stations were common. Some states called up the National Guard to help maintain control as desperate people do desperate things. The National Guard didn't help. It fell into disarray. Just driving to the grocery store was became dangerous. You needed to carry a gun for safety or your trip to the store could end up being your last.

Our currency became worthless due to inflation and the government closed all the banks to stop bank runs. A loaf of bread rose to $100 and milk to $150 per gallon, if you can find it. People have run out of money and even if they have any in the bank, they cannot take it out. The banks are closed. Savings accounts are wiped out and if you have any gold or silver in the bank forget it, the government took it. The government is taking everything because the country is bankrupt.

For many years illegal aliens have been coming across the border from Mexico. But not all the people are hardworking Mexicans looking for work. The fact is many of those crossing the border are from the Middle East and are related to Islamic radical terrorist groups. How do I know this? Because the US Government has admitted that every year several thousand manage to sneak into the USA.

The gangs and cartels that smuggle dope are also making inroads into the US selling their crap to whatever idiots will buy it. These gangs have turf wars and during their wars they don't care whom they rob or kill. Then there is the drug users who robs and kills to get money to pay for their habit. Finally we have the radical groups like the Skinheads, Neo-Nazis, some extremely violent religious people, and those that want white supremacy.

The government is now controlling the food and there are food lines at government controlled stores. You must wait for hours to get any food. If you can buy any food it is only enough for a few days. You cannot feed your family on a loaf of bread. Fresh vegetables and fruit cannot be found. Everything is canned goods or freeze dried ready to eat meals.

The question is can we change what we have become? There is no country to help us as they all have failed. We are the last hope of free mankind. We cannot forget the Bill of Rights, the United States Constitution, and the fact we are One Nation under God.

Here on Tocabaga we grow all our own food in a forty-acre garden. We found that we could grow almost any type of vegetable or fruit. Tocabaga has a chicken farm that provides eggs and chickens to our group. Most of our protein comes from eating fish. We have forty people that fish everyday to provide about 500 pounds a day to feed our group. We also have crabs, clams, and oysters that we harvest most of the year.

Everyone on Tocabaga works or has a job function to perform. If you don't work you don't eat. We have farmers, fishing crews, cooks, and lawn crews to fight back the fast growing jungle. We have auto mechanics and repairmen that can fix anything that breaks down. Most important of all we have 96 trained security people along with twenty Amazon Warriors who act as our police force. Everyone knows their job but each group has a lead man or supervisor that directs daily activities. The supervisors' meet once a week to coordinate activities for the whole island.

We have a Board of Directors made up of 12 members who have been elected by the people living here. The board members are elected every four years. The Board votes on all matters affecting the well-being of Tocabaga. Majority vote wins any debate and it cannot be voted on again for another year.

Most people living on Tocabaga carry a weapon. It's normal and totally expected to carry a gun because our second amendment rights permit us to do so. The only people that have been killed here were traitors. We do not tolerate traitors, spies, or Quislings. We all have a few things in common and that is the desire to remain free from Federal Government oppression and to protect our loved ones and friends.

I am the oldest of three brothers. We grew up fighting bullies and gang members in a tough neighborhood in south Chicago. My Dad, one of the most honest men I have known, always stressed, tell the truth, and help each other. Never ever be a bully, never steal, and try to protect those who cannot protect themselves. I have always stood up for the people who could not defend themselves. I hate liars and bullies.

Standing 6 feet tall at 180 pounds, I am in great shape for my age and my body is honed by years of physical training. I keep in shape by lifting weights almost every day and running three miles four times a week. I shave my head two times a week as it is cooler in the hot south and wear a ball hat to keep the sun off my head. The only hair on my head is a gray mustache and goatee that I keep well trimmed and short.

There is a two inch scar on my forehead from a knife fight years ago. I spent four years in the Army as a Military Policeman, and became an expert in the use of handguns, rifles, shotguns, and hand-to-hand combat. My legs have skin grafts from burns due to an explosion when working for the DOD (Department of Defense) doing security work for seven years. I always carry my Glock 17 side arm and Black Bear Cold Steel fighting knife.

I love our country, freedom, my family, and friends. If anyone messes with my family, or my friends, justice will be swift and painful. I have no use for anyone who breaks the law, cheats or steals. For the most part I follow the Ten Commandments, but also believe in The Code of Hammurabi which is an eye for an eye. I fight to keep our Bill of Rights under the United States Constitution.

That is me, Jack Gunn, a.k.a. Tocabaga Jack, and these are my chronicles.

I am Director of Security for Tocabaga Island. I live here along with 556 other Patriots. We are fighting to keep our freedom, keep our homes, and keep our families safe from the evil forces gone wild. Tocabaga is a sanctuary or safe haven. If you believe in the Constitution, the Bill of Rights, and are of good moral character you are welcome here.

We are waiting for you to contact us by email to find out where Tocabaga is located. Sending us an email is your first step to Freedom. There is an email address hidden in these chronicles. Tocabaga is a real location. I will reply.

THOMAS H. WARD

INTELLIGENCE BRIEF

A few days ago Jack Gunn and his crew terminated a total of 13 spies and Quislings with the help of the Androktones also called the Amazon Warriors. Maggie and Jack rescued Albert Madison's wife from a motorcycle gang leader named Buck. Maggie cut off Buck's arm and head, using her Barong Machete, killing the dork on the spot.

The Rangers assigned to Tocabaga were redeployed to fight the Federal Police Force thereby leaving Tocabaga without any Ranger security for a few days.

Jack let a group of twenty people enter the Tocabaga sanctuary. They claimed to be political prisoners who were being held at the Dome prison. Some of them turned out to be undercover Federal officers.

Stan Gill and Ken Johnson are two of the US Marshals who infiltrated Tocabaga and captured Jack. They also kidnapped little ten year old Johnny Evans. They planned to put Jack on trial for the murder of eight Federal agents killed by the Ellenton mob. The Marshals were taking Jack to Atlanta to face a firing squad. Fifteen miles later their SUV ran out of gas on Interstate 275 about half a mile before 54th Avenue North exit.

Stan advised Jack that his plan was to take over Tocabaga, turn it into a green zone, and boot the Army out. He said that Federal Police Troops would be arriving at Tocabaga in a few days.

Ken went to look for gas but never came back. Stan was killed by a sniper's bullet while standing next to the bullet proof Federal SUV. Jack and Johnny were stranded on the road side.

Jack, concerned for Johnny, decided to stay put in the bullet proof SUV rather than make a run for it in the darkness. There was no telling what they could run into in the danger zone. The danger zone is anywhere outside of Tocabaga. Jack was only armed with a Glock 9 mm containing 17 rounds.

As a group of people approached out of the darkness Jack got ready for the fight of his life.

Jack's only concern was to protect his grandson little Johnny.

NEW INTEL UPDATE

SOCOM intelligence advised a new threat is headed to Pinellas County. A warlord named BOKO KANG, a.k.a. THE DRAGON. Army Drones spotted his three hundred man army crossing the Howard Franklin Bridge two days ago.

THOMAS H. WARD

RECAP:

JULY 1, 2025

BEFORE MIDNIGHT

Johnny and I had been captured by U. S. Marshals who were taking me to Atlanta to be put on trial for the murder of eight Federal agents. The agents were actually killed by the mob at Ellenton.

We were about a half mile from the 54th Avenue exit on Interstate 275 when the motor sputtered and we rolled to a stop on the side of the highway. Stan asked Ken, "What's wrong?"

"Shit we're out of gas," Ken muttered.

"You dumb ass why didn't you check it? Get your butt out and go find some gas or another car. Hurry up! We'll wait here."

I knew Ken had a long walk ahead of him in a dangerous part of the city. I watched him walk north toward 54th Avenue at a fast pace until he disappeared into the darkness. I checked the time it was 9:30 pm.

I asked Stan, "Who are the other people that came to Tocabaga with you?"

Stan replied with a smirk on his face, "Wouldn't you like to know."

"Yes, I'd like to know. I'm going to be dead soon what difference does it make."

"Ok I'll tell you some of them were prisoners from the Dome but most of them are undercover Federal agents who are going to take over Tocabaga. We're going to make it a green zone and boot the Army out. The plans have been made and Federal Police will be arriving there in a few days."

"The FPF already attempted to take over Tocabaga but that failed. A lot of them were killed."

"That was only because you had the Rangers there. They won't be there this time to save your butts. I planned this whole thing. You're so easy to fool. Where the hell is Ken, he's been gone two hours?"

We were sitting there for another hour waiting for Ken to return with gas when Johnny said, "I gotta pee."

Stan opened the truck door got out and said, "Ok kid, go pee over there in the grass." Johnny got out and took a few steps to the grass. Stan was standing near him when I heard it.

A bullet whizzed by Stan and then another, one hit him in the torso knocking him to the ground. Stan let out a groan as he fell and then was silent. I shouted to Johnny, "Quick! Come here and untie me!"

Johnny climbed in the truck and untied my hands. I jumped out and grabbed Stan's handgun, which happened to be one of my Glocks. I checked his pulse, he was dead. Climbing back into the bullet proof SUV I wondered who shot Stan.

A Glock is without a doubt the best handgun ever made. The barrels never wear out and they are very dependable. It will fire under water, you can throw it in the mud, or run it over with a truck, and it still works every time. It is light weight and has a 17 round magazine capacity. The luger 9mm round is the most common handgun ammunition. It's used by the military and police departments all over the United States.

Tommy never misses. His motto is one shot one kill. I concluded the shooter couldn't have been Tommy because he doesn't miss. The question is who shot Stan?

I locked all the doors as Johnny peered out the windows looking for the shooter. Johnny said, "Look, Grandpa, some people are coming this way."

Looking out the windshield I saw them, a group of people, coming towards us out of the darkness. The people were too far away to make out who they were. I could only see dark shadow-like figures walking slowly in our direction.

I looked out the back window and there were more people coming from behind us. I thought oh no, FUBAR! Are these gang people, Federal Police, or who?

Johnny asked, "What do we do now Grandpa?"

"Don't worry, Johnny, they can't break into this bullet-proof truck. Just keep your head down and Grandpa will take care of it." Grandpa was very worried to say the least.

I rolled up all the windows and pulled down the inside sun shades to cover them. I smashed the interior lights so the door could be opened without lighting up the interior thereby making us easy targets.

I said a prayer, "God do what you will with me, but please protect little Johnny from evil."

Checking my gun to insure there was a round in the chamber, I waited as they approached. With only 17 rounds I didn't stand a chance. I looked again and both groups where within 200 Yards. They were slowly closing in on us one step at a time.

JULY 2, 2025

JUST AFTER MIDNIGHT

It was past midnight as the people with questionable intentions approached our vehicle. Johnny asked, "Are they still coming Grandpa?"

Lifting up a window shade I replied, "Yep, they're still coming, but don't worry Grandpa will take care of everything." Johnny was sitting on the floor, next to my legs, his hands tightly holding on to me. I cracked a couple of windows open because it was getting hot inside the SUV. I was sweating like a pig.

A blanket was covering something in the back storage area so I slowly pulled it off and there was my M4 carbine with 300 rounds of ammo. Someone must have put it in the back when Maggie and I went to rescue Sue. I had forgotten all about the gun, because so much had happened yesterday. At least now I had a fighting chance.

The gangs reached the truck and someone tried to open the door. One man said, "This is a Federal truck. The door is locked. Joe, this guy here is dead. Nice shooting."

They tried all the other doors. Then a person yelled, "You in the truck, come out now! Throw out your guns and come out with your hands in the air!"

He yelled again, "Come on out of the truck. We know you're in there. If you don't come out we'll blow it up or start it on fire! Come out now!"

I didn't think of that, they could start the truck on fire. An explosion badly burned my body years ago. Getting burned to death is a long painful process. There were about forty people were standing around the truck. That's too many to fight so we'll have to face the danger.

I told Johnny, "I'm going to open the door and get out."

"Ok, if you say so... but don't get killed Grandpa." Johnny reached out and touched my hand as if to say I trust you.

"We're coming out so don't shoot. I'm throwing out my guns."

Opening the side back door I threw out the guns and stepped out with my arms in the air. Johnny was holding on to my waist. A couple of guys grabbed me and tied my hands behind my back.

Another one grabbed Johnny asking, "Joe, should I tie up the kid?"

The man named Joe replied, "No need."

Joe put his face up close to mine. He was a mean looking dude with bad breath and stained teeth. He asked, "Who the hell are y'all? Are you a Fed?" He looked me right in the eye to see if I was telling him the truth.

Joe stood about six-foot-two and probably weighted around 230 pounds. He had on a black tank top and army cargo type pants. I could tell he was in pretty good shape by the toned muscles in his arms. I guessed his age to be in the late twenties or early thirties. His nose was crooked which meant it had been broken a few times.

"I'm not a Fed. I'm Jack Gunn and this is my Grandson Johnny. You know, you could use a Tic Tac." He backed off a step while pointing his AK47 at me.

"That's very funny, old man. Tell me what are you doing in a Fed truck?"

"They arrested me for killing eight Federal Agents and kidnapped my grandson, holding him as a hostage, in case I tried anything stupid. He's the Fed," while nodding my head towards Stan's body.

Joe bent down, frisked his body, and said, "He ain't got a badge or ID on him."

"Believe me he's a US Marshal and there was another one with us. We ran out of gas and he went to find some about four hours ago."

"Where were they taking you?"

"Atlanta."

One man got in the driver's seat and tried to start the engine and I said, "I told you it's out of gas."

Joe told him, "Russell, go get some gas and then bring the truck back to the Boss Man."

"Ok, old man let's go, we'll find out if your story is true."

He gave me a push in the direction of 54th Avenue and Johnny held on to me. The group was a ragtag band made up of women and men. I thought maybe this is the 54th Avenue Gang that controls the north side of St. Petersburg. They don't like the Feds any-more than I do.

I had heard about the 54th Avenue Gang from Army Ranger Intel reports. They number a few hundred people and where controlled by one man named Big Boss. The gang kept the Feds out of the area along with other evil-doers. The problem was they controlled all the food and supplies. People were forced to pay for protection and goods. If you didn't pay you were banished from the area or terminated.

We walked toward 54th Avenue in the dark hot night. Sweat was running down my face. Johnny asked me, "Where are they taking us?"

"I don't know but we'll find out soon."

A woman from the group walked up holding out a bottle and asked, "Hey, kid, you want some water?"

Johnny looked at me and I looked at her noting her short brown hair surrounding her dirty, but kind looking face. She appeared to be in her late twenties and was dressed in tight short-shorts showing off her butt. The halter top barely covered her breasts. Combat boots made her long shapely legs stand out. She was about five feet six and in great shape.

Looking in her eyes I could tell she had some Asian blood running through her veins and I asked, "Is that really water?"

"Of course, it is Mister. We have rules here and one rule is we don't hurt kids.

"Here, you taste it." Putting it to my lips she poured some in my mouth. She was so close her breasts lightly brushed up against my body.

"Johnny, it's ok." We hadn't had anything to drink for about six hours.

"You don't trust anyone do you?" she asked.

"Thanks for the water, but I'm just looking out for my grandson."

"I told you nothing is gonna happen to him. My name is Lisa."

"I'm Jack, and this is, Johnny."

"Hi, Johnny, you want some more water?"

"Yes, please." Lisa pulled out another bottle and while handing it to Johnny she patted him on the head.

"Jack, you don't need to worry if something happens … to you … I'll take care of Johnny."

"Thanks Lisa, but nothing is gonna happen."

"Are you a tough guy, Jack? You look like one to me. You got nice big arms. You look strong and tough. Anyway, you're gonna need to be tough."

"Why is that?"

"You'll see soon enough. Just worry about

yourself and remember what I told you.

"We captured another guy earlier who told us you're a Fed. He said Johnny was his grandson."

"That has to be Ken. He's a liar obviously. Johnny will tell you that."

"I can tell Johnny's your grandson."

Joe yelled, "Lisa, stop talking to him!"

"Shut up, I'll do what I want." We kept walking but the conversation ended.

We reached 54th and turned east for a few blocks until we reached 16th Street and the old Northeast High School. They took us to a room in the main school building, opened the door, and pushed us inside. "See you later Johnny. You, too Jack," Lisa said, as she closed the door.

I told Johnny, "Untie my hands."

I checked the door, but it was locked much to my regret. I looked around the room as my eyes adjusted to the dark. There were no lights or windows. My eyes slowly adjusted to the darkness. I saw a person sitting in the corner of the room and slowly walked over to him. I balled my hands into a fist getting ready to fight whoever it was.

I stopped a few feet away when I saw it was Ken. He said, "Hi Jack, where's Stan?"

"Stan is dead and so are you." I reached down and grabbed him by the shirt pulling him to his feet. I put my hands around his throat and started to squeeze.

"Wait, I was just doing my job. Stan made me do it. He made me be a part of the whole dirty thing. If I didn't go along with him he'd lock me up again. I think we can help each other and escape from this hole," Ken begged me.

"Maybe you're right, you lying little weasel. I won't kill you yet."

"What do you think they're going to do to us?"

"I don't know, but we'll find out pretty soon."

I went to the other side of the twenty foot room moving as far away from Ken as possible. We didn't say another word to each other. Johnny and I laid down on the hard floor. He used my shoulder as a pillow and fell fast asleep. Looking at my watch it was five a.m. as I fell into a light sleep while keeping one eye on Ken.

"Hey, wake up you guys," Lisa, said in a stern voice. Johnny and I jumped up and saw Joe and four men were standing next to her.

"Johnny, are you hungry?" Johnny nodded

his head yes. "Ok let's go eat."

Lisa looked even better in the daylight. She was all cleaned up, but still had on the same outfit. I couldn't stop looking at her cute little ass and great shapely legs.

We followed her, while the four men kept their guns pointed at our backs, to the school cafeteria. "You got a choice of Spam or Spam and beans," Lisa told us while laughing.

There were other people in the room and some of them stared at us as we walked in. It was a busy place with people coming in to eat. Everyone carried some type of weapon.

"I'll have Spam and beans," Johnny said.

"Same for me," I replied.

Smart ass Ken said, "Not much choice here at the Hilton. I'll have the same." I thought we're lucky to get anything to eat.

Lisa made sure Johnny had enough to eat and drink. The meal was crude by our standards on Tocabaga. Eating just beans and Spam with no fruit or other vegetables wasn't very healthy, but it was filling.

It was hot and judging by the bright sun it was around noon. We finished eating and Lisa advised us, "Ok, it's time to meet the BIG BOSS.

Let's get going he's waiting for us."

Following her Johnny held onto my hand as we walked to what was once the gym. High school kids used to play basketball and other indoor sports in the gym. Passing through the metal doors I saw him sitting at the other end of the big room.

He was sitting in a big throne like chair, up on a pedestal, above everyone else. There were about a dozen people standing or sitting around him in a semi circle. The room was smoky and smelled like pot and cigarettes. As we approached I could make him out in the shadows. I could see his shape and noted he didn't have a shirt on. His body was covered in tribal tattoos and so was his face. He was a huge hunk of muscle with a massive chest and thick Herculean arms.

We stopped about fifteen feet away from him and I could clearly see his face. One man, who looked like a little rat, ran up to us and said, "Kneel before the BIG BOSS."

Ken knelt down to the BOSS. I didn't and I saw the little rat's fist coming out of the corner of my eye. I quickly raised my left hand and grabbed his arm stopping it in mid-air. I pulled him up close to me. Using my right hand I seized his thumb and bent it backwards in a counter-clock wise direction until I heard it snap.

The little rat screamed, "You broke my thumb! The asshole broke my thumb!"

BIG BOSS chuckled out loud and told him, "Sit down you fool. You're lucky he didn't break your neck."

Another guy, standing next to BIG BOSS, shouted, "Let me take this guy out!"

"You can't take him out. He'd beat your ass with no problem, so sit down and shut up!"

He asked, "Do you know this guy, BIG BOSS?"

"Yeah, that's Jack Gunn. Now everybody get out of here! I want to talk to Jack alone. Lisa, take the kid outside to play. Joe, take Ken back to the room and lock him up."

Johnny looked up at me and I said, "It's ok, go with Lisa."

Lisa walked up to BOSS and gave him a big wet kiss. It was clear they had a thing for each other. I watched her leave the room with Johnny holding her hand.

In a few minutes the big room was empty. I looked at the BOSS as he stepped down from his throne and out into the light. His face and body were covered with black ink tattoos. His head was shaved into a short Mohawk haircut. He had muscles alright and I knew he took roids to be that big. BOSS stood almost six feet and looked to be about 240 pounds of solid muscle. I knew he was in his early fifties.

He stood there looking me up and down with a grin on his face and said, "Hello Jack, long-time no see. How have you been?"

"Hello Rico, or should I call you … BOSS."

"Come on Jack, I'm Rico to you, we go back a long way. I thought you were dead. I read on the internet that al-Qaida killed you."

"They tried to, but I'm still around."

"Yeah, you're one tough old fart. I didn't think al-Qaida could kill you. Who's the kid with you?"

"That's my grandson, Johnny."

Miguel (Mike) Rico Martin, ex-Navy Seal, ex-Swat Captain, one of the toughest men I have ever known was now the BIG BOSS of the 54th Avenue Gang.

Rico and I go back a long way. I first met him while at the shooting range in Tampa. We were shooting the same model handgun, a Glock 17, and had lanes next to each other. I didn't know who he was but I could tell by his form and style he had some type of military training. I commented to him on his nice shooting.

We shook hands and started talking and we became friends right off the bat. I came to find out that he was the SWAT Team Captain for a local police department. He was booted out of the Navy after fifteen years for striking an officer. Eight of those years he was assigned to Special Operations. No telling what he really did during those years because he never spoke of it.

One thing for sure, Rico Martin was an operator who knew his stuff. I knew him like a book. He is the most dangerous man I know. He's a one man killing machine.

"Come on over here and sit down. You want a beer?"

As I sat down at the table he walked over to a cooler and pulled out two beers advising me, "The beer isn't ice cold, but it's still good."

We popped the tops and I made a toast. "Here's to old friends."

"To old friends, it's nice to see you again."

"Rico, what happen to you when the country fell apart? How's your wife and son?"

"Well it's a long story, but my wife and son

are gone. I don't know where they're at. The Feds kidnapped them because I wouldn't do their dirty work. They tried to get me to work undercover to round up the so called rebels, like you, who weren't co-operating with big brother."

We both took a long chug of beer and he hung his head down looking at the floor as if thinking what to say.

"Any-how I refused to do their dirty work. Then one day I came home from work and my family was gone. The Feds left a note; *if you want to see your family again then join us.*"

"I'm sorry Rico. The Feds will do anything. They're a bunch of scum bags. We knew the country was falling apart that's why we practiced shooting every week. That's why we stored ammo and food. That's why we started the fight club."

Twenty years ago Fight Club was Rico's big idea. We would meet once a week at a local gym and trained in hand-to-hand combat. Rico wrote the book on hand-to-hand combat; and on knife fighting. It was Rico who gave me the Cold Steel Black Bear fighting knife. All Warriors' carry at least one knife. He taught the members of our fight club, honing our skills, in advanced fighting methods. He tried to mold us into his image of a

Warrior.

We would have combat sparring sessions which were painful but it made you better and tougher. No one ever beat Rico in five years of training. We practiced knife fighting using eight inch long hard rubber knives which hurt like hell if you got stuck or sliced. Sometimes they would draw blood.

The only time I ever beat Rico at was a three gun shoot. A three gun shoot is shooting at targets with a handgun, shotgun, and a rifle. We entered the Tampa Bay Annual 3 GUN SHOOT and I won the contest, out-shooting Rico by one bull's eye.

I asked him, "After they took your wife, what did you do?"

"I went on a killing spree. I used all my skill to kill every Federal Agent I could find. They put a one million dollar bounty on my head. I'm wanted dead or alive. I searched for my wife and son but couldn't find them.

"I had to keep moving because they were after me every day. I ended up here about three years ago and started this group to maintain control of the area and to provide me some protection. I needed my own little army."

"You should have come to Tocabaga."

"I know, but I wouldn't fit in there. I am a womanizer, and an alpha male. I give orders. I don't take them. I can't follow anyone, not even you.

"Do you still have the Black Bear I gave you?"

A good fighting knife has a one piece shank and blade. It is made of hardened steel with a softer inner core but the blade edge is hard and sharp as a razor blade. Fighting knifes have a finger hook or sub hilt for your index finger to wrap around and a hand guard to keep your fingers from getting cut off. The nice thing about the Black Bear knife manufactured by Cold Steel is that both edges are sharp as a razor so you can slice and dice in either direction.

"Yep, it saved my life. I killed two al-Qaida guys' with it by slitting their stinking throats. I carry it everywhere I go."

"How did you get here and who's Ken?"

"To make a long story short Ken is a US Marshal and there was another one named Stan, who was the leader, but your people killed him. Stan and Ken managed to arrest me and held

Johnny as hostage so I wouldn't try to escape."

BOSS pulled out a pack of smokes and offered me one. I took a long deep drag, and blew out a perfect white smoke ring.

Looking at Rico, I said, "They arrested me for killing eight agents at Ellenton. They were taking me to Atlanta when the SUV ran out of gas. Then your gang found us. End of story."

"Did you kill the Agents?"

"No not really. We took their guns and SUVs. Then a mob of people at Ellenton chased them down and shot them."

"Serves them right … they got We The People justice. How many bad guys have you killed?"

I laughed and replied, "Between the Feds and dope heads I don't have any idea. What about you?"

BOSS looked up in the air for a second or two and said, "I don't know, at least a couple of hundred. You know you're going to have to kill that Marshal."

I didn't say a word because I knew Ken was already dead. If I didn't kill him then Rico would make him suffer before he killed him. It was better for Ken if I did him in.

Rico commented, "I should have lived in the Roman times. I would have made a great Gladiator. I hate to tell you this, but I enjoy the killing and inflicting pain on those I hate. I love everything about combat."

Now I knew that Rico had gone over the edge. He has so much hate in him that he has turned to the dark side. I looked at his face and thought I saw the devil in his eyes. It sent a chill down my spine.

"Tomorrow is Friday and that's fight night. We have a tradition here that on Friday night someone fights. Sometimes it's a fight to the death. That's our entertainment. What we do is capture any invaders who cross into our territory. They're the people we normally fight. We give them fair warning by nailing posters to the light poles stating; '*NO TRESPASSING - Enter 54th Ave. at your own risk.*' The sign has a skull and cross bones painted on it.

"Sometimes we let them go, after a good beating, so they can warn their friends to keep out. If they win the fight they can leave or join us. I call my group of warriors the DIMACHAERUS CLAN.

"I want you to fight Ken to the death Gladiator style. Have you ever heard of the DIMACHAERUS?"

"No. I've never heard of them."

"They lived in Roman times and would fight in the arena, with no armor, using knives or swords. When you fight I'll let you use my Black Bear." He patted the knife hanging on his hip.

I wondered how many men Rico had killed with the Cold Steel blade.

"Rico, why don't you just let Johnny and me leave? I don't want to kill Ken. He's not much of a challenge. You do what you want with him."

BOSS stood up and walked around in a circle looking down at the floor. Then he stopped and looked up at the ceiling and said, "Jack, you just got here and I can't let you leave. If you want to leave you'll have to fight your way out."

"Fight my way out! What the hell do you mean?"

"Here's the deal. I agree with you, fighting Ken is not much of a challenge. Lisa will fight Ken and after she kills him then anyone of my men can call you out."

"What if I don't accept?"

"You must accept the fight or be killed on the spot. It's kill or be killed just like the Roman Dimachaerus."

"You're gonna let Lisa knife fight. That's

crazy!"

"Man, she's good. I've been training her for three years. She already killed four men in the ring. Lisa is fast and knows all the tricks. I'll bet you she kills Ken in less than three minutes."

"I only terminate bad guys that are trying to kill me or my family. You're killing for fun."

"Jack, we are the bad guys. You have no choice."

One of the big rusty metal doors squeaked opened and in walked Lisa with Johnny. Lisa looked strong and in great shape. Her arm and leg muscles were well defined.

Lisa asked, "Are you two done talking yet?"

BOSS commented, "Not yet. What's up?"

"I thought you should know Hank was bugging little Johnny, asking him a lot questions."

I asked, "Who the hell is Hank?"

"He's an admitted pervert, but he has never bothered any of the kids living here," replied Rico.

"You let a pervert near your kids?"

"He didn't do anything or I would have killed him. He just rubbed Johnny on top of the head," Lisa advised.

"That's it! Jack, you can fight Hank. Kill him if you like. He's a worthless piece of shit anyway," BOSS said.

"Ok, you got your fight. After I kill this pervert we're out of here."

"Hank is no push over. He's a tall lean fast guy. Not as strong as you but I think he's faster than you. Why are you in such a hurry to leave?"

"Look you don't understand, my people will be looking for me. I don't want a war between our groups. If they think you're holding me against my will there'll be trouble for sure."

"How many people you got?"

"I have enough people to match your ragtag group. They're fully trained and well armed. We also have two BFVs'."

The Bradley M3 Fighting Vehicle (BFV) is named after General Omar Bradley from WWII. The BFV is operated by a three man crew and is fully armored. It can transport up to six fully armed combat ready men. For weapon power it fires a 25mm chain gun which can destroy most tanks and has a 7.62 M240 machine gun.

"If you got Bradleys then that's another

story. Where the hell did you get those from?"

"There's a Platoon of Rangers based at Fort Desoto. They control the BFVs' and an Abrams tank that protect Tocabaga and the Ranger base."

"Shit, you got some serious fire power. Ok, here's the deal. You and the kid can leave anytime you want after the fight tomorrow, but I keep the SUV."

"That's fine with me. I just wanna get back to Tocabaga and take care of my family."

Knowing Rico, I knew it wasn't going to be that easy. He was going to try and pull some kind of shit. He has a giant ego and always wants to be in the limelight.

Rico commented, "Come with me and I'll show you around. I built this place so we could defend it. I have two hundred and twenty people here. One hundred of them are fighters. The others provide support functions."

Lisa and Johnny tagged along behind us. It was a bright sunny hot day with a clear blue sky.

We went outside to review the perimeter of the school grounds and I asked, "How much territory do you control?"

"We go wherever we like but no one is permitted inside our security zone. The zone goes west to Interstate 275 and east to 9th Avenue. The north limit is 62nd Avenue and south is 46th Avenue. That's the area we can safely defend. We patrol the zone 24-7."

"How do you obtain your food and supplies?"

"We forage, steal, or do whatever is necessary to obtain what we want. Some of the men and women go fishing. We have a small garden and also raise chickens. One of our men trapped some rabbits and we'll try to raise them. The body needs a lot of protein to maintain muscle mass."

"Raising rabbits is a good idea. On Tocabaga they run wild and we hunt them."

The school property had about ten buildings and it was all surrounded by a twelve foot high chain-link fence with razor wire on the top. There was only one way in which was through the main class room building. Rico had four M2 50 caliber machine gun nests, one on each corner, located inside the fence. At the main door he had sand bag fortifications and two men on guard armed with light M249 machine guns.

The M2 heavy machine gun is a 50 caliber Browning machine gun (BMG) round that can go through steel, even an engine block. It can go

33

through one side of a car, come out the other side, and still kill someone. The BMG has a muzzle velocity of 1,900 miles per hour or 2,800 feet per second. The BMG bullet is a ½-inch in diameter and nearly 4 inches long. I call it the Superman Bullet.

A SAW M249 is a light machine gun that fires a 5.56 NATO round up to 700 rounds per minute. It is an awesome weapon that can be moved very quickly. You need 2 men to carry all the ammo this baby fires. It is belt fed or uses 100 round drums. The effective range is 600 yards.

There were sandbag emplacements in between the machine guns and they were all connected by a line of trenches. Using the trench network forces could move from one position to another without getting shot.

I noticed the buildings themselves were made of brick and concrete block. They all had steel doors and the windows had a thick metal mesh screen covering them. I was impressed with the whole layout. Rico had done a good job turning this school into a fortress. It would hold up well against small arms fire but not against heavy weapons like a tank.

I told Rico, "Good job on your defensive

network. It's impressive to say the least. What type of weapons do you have besides the machine guns?"

"Our assault rifles are mostly AK47s'. We have some pineapples and a few RPGs. I put some claymore mines around the perimeter."

An AK47 fires a 7.62 x 39mm round. It is an assault rifle developed in the old Soviet Union by Mikhail Kalashnikov in 1947. Officially it is called the Auto Kalashnikov hence AK47. It is the weapon of choice for terrorists since it is cheap and readily available. Worldwide more of these guns were produced than any other type. It is a sturdy rifle and dangerous at close range but it is not very accurate.

A rocket-propelled grenade (RPG) is a weapon system that fires rockets equipped with a war head that explodes. They are very dangerous for ground troops, can shoot down choppers, and also stop tanks if the correct type of war head is used.

The Pineapple is a M67 hand grenade. It is a small bomb that can be thrown by hand. It's designed to detonate after a set amount of time, usually about 4 seconds. The M67 is an anti-personnel fragmentation grenade that disperses lethal fragments upon detonation. If you're within a few meters then kiss your ass good-bye.

Internally an M18A1 Claymore mine contains C4 explosives and a layer of seven hundred $\frac{1}{8}$-inch-diameter steel balls set into an epoxy resin. When it is detonated, the explosion drives the steel balls forward, out of the mine. The steel balls are projected in a 60° fan-shaped pattern that is 6.5 feet high and 55 yards wide at a range of 150 feet. A very effective killing weapon because one mine can kill or wound many men. It cuts them to pieces.

"Where'd you get that stuff from?"

"I still got connections with the police and military."

"I imagine you still do."

"Our big problem is food. Feeding this large group of people isn't easy."

"I think you need to increase the size of the garden and raise more chickens. Chickens lay eggs which are great protein and they provide meat. You could also have more people fishing. On Tocabaga we bring in 500 pounds of fish a day.

"What is your command structure and how does your internal political system function?"

"I have four Lieutenants' and eight Sergeants'. They all have some type of military experience. What do you mean by political system?"

Rico didn't like the word political. He doesn't want to share power with anyone.

I advised Rico, "You know the people who aren't fighters. The ones who do all the support work. Who's in charge of their activities?"

"I just tell everyone what to do. Believe me it is a full time job. I'm getting tired of it."

"Your people need to elect four or five leaders to head up the different support activities like fishing, gardening, hunting, and so forth. Then let people volunteer for a work group of their choice.

"You need to elect a Board of Directors made of six to twelve people."

"Jack, this isn't a Democracy. I'm the BOSS around here. I got the final word on everything."

"Ok, but to make your job easier let the people elect a head person for the different activities. That way you only have your four Lieutenants and four supervisors reporting to you."

"I got a better idea. I'll appoint them myself. If they don't do a good job then I can fire them."

"Ok, whatever you say. You need to set goals for the support groups so you don't run out of food. I would let them elect their own leaders. They know better than you who's the best at what they do."

"Why don't you stick around and help me out. You could handle that for me."

I looked up at the sky and then at the ground thinking how to answer him.

"Sorry, Rico, I can't do that."

"You mean you don't want to help out an old buddy."

"I'm needed on Tocabaga."

Rico stood there for a few minutes, folded his arms, and looked down at the ground. I could tell he was thinking what to say.

"Jack, do you think I'm crazy?"

"You're not crazy, just a little mixed up. The Feds screwed up your head when they took your family. That would screw up my brain. Tell you what I'll do for you. I'll come here one day a week with some of my people and help set up a system. I have excellent farmers and other good people that can teach your group."

Lisa commented, "That sounds like a good idea. Don't you think so, Rico?"

"Yes, it's a good idea and I appreciate your offer."

Rico stopped and pointed, "Here's our garden area. We just increased the size. We do need help to improve the amount of crops we grow."

I looked at the small garden and there were about ten people working the field. One man, with a straw hat on, dropped what he was doing and started walking towards us. He was lean looking and in good shape. He took off his hat showing his red clown-like hair.

The red headed man walked up and said, "Hi Johnny," and touched Johnny's head. I knew instantly that he was the pervert Hank.

I seized his arm and growled at him in a low voice, "Touch the kid again, and I'll kill you!"

The pervert replied, "You mean like this," and he touched Johnny on the head again. Now my blood was boiling and I had to kill him. There is nothing I hate more than a child molester.

I was getting ready to grab him by the throat when he suddenly drew his handgun and pointed it at me. Fast as lighting Rico snatched it from his hand and hit him in the face with the barrel knocking him down. Blood was running from his nose.

As he stood up Rico told him, "I'll give this back to you later. For pulling that gun, you're going to fight Jack to the death tomorrow night. Now get the hell away from us before I kill you myself."

Hank hung his head down as he started to walk away, but then he hesitated, looked at me, and hissed, "You're a dead man walking. I'll get the kid after I kill you."

Rico calmly said, "Ok, that did it. You should kill him now, Jack," as he handed me his Black Bear.

Johnny shouted, "Look out Grandpa. He's got a knife!"

Lisa pulled Johnny aside, out of the way, as Hank lunged at me with a knife in his left hand. I turned sideways while jumping back and the blade just missed slicing open my gut.

The thrust threw Hank off balance putting his back directly in line with my right hand. I stabbed him in the back, on the left side, right below the shoulder blade with all my might knocking him to the ground face first.

Then I stomped on his knife hand and he yelped as his hand or fingers broke. Smashing his hand again, with my combat boot, I kicked the knife away. He was flopping around trying to get up so I dropped down, with all my weight, ramming my right knee into his spine.

He let out a groan as the wind got knocked out of him. Sitting on his back he couldn't move as I forced his head down. I quickly shoved the sharp tip of my blade into the base of his skull, where the spinal cord connects to the brain stem, and rammed it home with all my strength. In a second his body went limp.

I sat there on his back for a minute to gain back my breath. The fight was over in less than a minute and Rico commented, "Jack that was a thing of beauty. For an old man you still got what it takes," as he helped me get back on my feet.

I wiped the blade off on Hank's shirt and gave it back to Rico. "Thanks Rico, but I'm slowing down. The pervert would have killed me if it wasn't for Johnny.

"Good job Johnny you saved Grandpa's life." I was shaking from the fight because it used all my strength and energy up.

"Don't worry I got your back, Grandpa." We all laughed at that comment, but it was true.

Lisa was holding onto Johnny keeping his eyes away from the bloody body. We walked away from the dead child molester, as other people ran up to observe what was going on.

Rico told one man, "Get rid of his body."

I heard someone say, "That new guy just killed the pervert."

Another one replied, "Good, I'm glad he's dead."

I thought how could Rico let people like that into his clan.

"Lisa, give Jack back his guns. I trust him one hundred percent. He doesn't have to fight tomorrow since he just killed Hank," Rico advised.

"Jack, I'd like you to stay tonight to obtain a better idea of how we operate. Maybe you'll stay tomorrow to watch Lisa fight."

Lisa, while holding on to my arm, said, "Jack, please stay. You can help Rico out and watch me fight. Who am I fighting, Rico?"

"Ken the Marshal."

"Alright, we'll stay tonight, but after the fight tomorrow we have to leave. I promise to come back to help you organize your group."

That night, a few hours after a dinner of grilled squirrel, peppers, and greens, everyone went to the meeting hall or gymnasium. Rico sat on his throne and I observed from the side lines with Johnny. Sitting next to Rico, on his right was Lisa, and to his left was Joe. I assumed that Joe must be his second-in-command. Behind Rico sat his four Lieutenants and everyone carried guns.

It was getting dark and the room was lit up by the flickering flames of smoking torches. The skylight windows in the ceiling were open to let the heat and smoke out. The room was hot and the body odor was strong.

I looked at Johnny and he was sweating. Johnny held his nose and commented, "It stinks in here."

There were, by my estimate, about one hundred people jammed into the room. Joe spoke up, "This meeting is in order!" Then he slammed a big hammer to the ground … Bam … Bam … Bam … and all was quiet.

"BIG BOSS will speak now," Joe shouted.

BOSS stayed seated and yelled, "Does anyone have any grievances?"

One man stood up and commented, "Yes, I want to complain about the food. There's not enough food and it tastes like shit."

Everyone in the room started to laugh, including me.

BOSS answered, "You say it tastes like shit. Then you don't have to eat it. That will leave more for others. You can find your own food from now on. Guards throw him out!"

"Are there any other grievances?"

A middle aged woman stood up and advised, "We need to have better clothes. All we have are rags to wear and old shoes."

"Ok, you're in charge of clothes from now on. Do whatever it takes to make everyone happy. By the way I want a new pair of pants. Have them ready by tomorrow."

Another person stood up, "BIG BOSS, we need a crew to keep the buildings and grounds clean."

"Ok, good idea. You're now in charge of daily clean up. Pick five people to help you."

"Are there any more grievances?"

One young man raised his hand and stood up. "My name is Jay, Sir. I'm a perimeter security guard. The problem is Big Les took my AK47."

"Les stand up!" BOSS shouted.

A man about six feet six inches tall stood up towering over everyone. In his huge hands the AK47 looked like a toy gun. He appeared to be around forty years old.

Rico asked him, "Did you steal his gun?"

"No, it's my gun. The little shit is a liar."

"Jay, can you prove it's your gun?"

"Yes Sir BOSS, my name is carved in the butt."

BOSS slowly rose out of his chair with Joe following behind him and walked up to Big Les. He held out his hand to take the AK and Les hesitated for a second, but handed over the gun. Rico looked at the butt and then handed the gun to Jay. You could feel the tension in the air as BOSS turned around looking at Les.

"Les you're guilty of stealing from a fellow clan member and lying to me about it. That's not good Les. That means we can't trust you," BOSS advised in a soft voice.

BOSS while turning around in circles he raised his arms high in the air. His arm muscles were flexing when he yelled, "I hereby sentence you to death!"

Then he quickly dropped both arms and, as if on cue, Joe swung the big five pound sledge hammer. You could hear the sickening thud of hard metal striking Les in the back of the head.

I grabbed Johnny, turned his head, and buried his face in my gut so he couldn't watch the brutal killing.

Les fell to the ground moaning as Joe struck

him again and again until his skull caved in. There was no doubt Les was dead. No one in the room made a noise, fearing they could be next on the Hit list.

Joe ordered, "Guards remove the body." Rico and Joe went back up to the throne and sat down.

BIG BOSS stated, "No more grievances for now. Let us hear the daily reports. Joe give the security report."

Joe stood up advising, "The patrol teams captured three male invaders today and one female. They're from the 38th Avenue gang. Invaders stand up and be recognized."

They stood up next to four guards in the corner of the room. The guards dragged them out into the center of the room. People started yelling, "Kill the invaders, kill the invaders!"

This was a real Kangaroo court. Rico was the judge and jury. He ran everything because everyone was afraid of him. He ruled by intimidation and fear. He was a bully and I don't like bullies.

BOSS yelled, "Everyone be quite! Invaders, why did you come into our territory?"

The woman spoke, "Sir, we came here in

peace searching for food and supplies, not to hurt anyone. We don't have any weapons."

Joe replied, "That's not true. One of the men had an AK47."

Rico answered, "Coming here for food is hurting us. We need all the food we can obtain. You are guilty of stealing and I sentence you to fight tomorrow night for your freedom. It'll be hand-to-hand, no weapons permitted. You'll fight one of my people. The first one to surrender is the loser. If you lose then you'll be sentenced to one year hard labor. If you win you can go free, but never come back into our territory again or it'll be the death sentence."

The woman prisoner spoke up again, "Sir, we aren't fighters. We're cooks, and if I may say, great cooks. We would like to stay here and improve your food quality since, one man commented, it tastes like shit."

"Do the other cooks feel the same way?"

"Yes Sir, we're cooks not fighters, they both agree with me," as she pointed towards two older men who looked like cooks. It was clear they were not in shape to fight anyone.

The fourth man in the group dressed in military style clothing spoke up and said, "Who do you think you are? God?" He spit on the floor towards BIG BOSS.

"What's your name big guy?" Rico leaned forward in his chair.

He answered, "Allen Jones."

"Allen, I am God here, and I hereby sentence you to fight to the death tomorrow. The three cooks can join our group and don't have to fight anyone. Cooks, you start tomorrow so it better be good.

"Guards assign them a room, in the main building, for the night. Lock up Allen in a different room and post a guard.

"Who has the Hunter Gather report?"

"I do BIG BOSS."

"Give me your daily report. What's your name again?"

"BOSS, I'm Billy. I'm sorry to report we didn't kill one animal today. Not even a bird, but we did manage to catch a few fish and pick a bucket of oranges."

Billy looked to be a kid about twenty years old. He was too young to know what was needed to feed all these people.

"Dam it! Billy, that's not good enough. We have two hundred people to feed. You take a crew of thirty men and go back out now. We need two hundred pounds of fish, ten buckets of oranges, and whatever else, you can gather. Stay out all night if needed. If you can't do the job better I'll fire you! You know what that means."

"Ok, I got it BOSS. I won't let you down." Billy quickly left the room with a few other men.

Rico's instructions didn't help him out. I knew obtaining two hundred pounds of fish was not easy task to do when fishing from shore. I assumed that getting fired meant being kicked out of the Clan.

"Next is the Farm report. Come on someone speak up," Rico commanded.

An older woman stood up and said, "That's me BIG BOSS. I have four dozen eggs and ten chickens for the killing. In addition we have five rabbits. We picked five buckets of carrots, three of beans, three buckets of berries, five of cucumbers, and five buckets of peppers.

"In addition we increased the garden size and we expect to double production in a few months."

"Finally someone who knows what they're doing. Good job, Emma."

With that BOSS yelled, "The meeting is

over!"

People slowly filed out of the room and Rico meandered over to me and asked, "Well, what do you think?"

I saw Joe the Hammer leave the room to wash the blood and brains off.

"I think you're lucky someone hasn't killed you by now. Some of it was good but some of it was out of line."

"I told you I'm the BOSS here and things are done my way. You didn't like Joe killing that guy, right. I needed to set an example for the new cooks and my people. No one steals from another clan member. If I let him get away with that then the whole clan could fall apart. Let's get a beer and have a smoke."

Rico looked at Johnny. "We got a special treat for you."

We sat down at a table along with Lisa. Rico inquired, "So tell me what kind of changes would you make, Jack?" Just then Joe walked up to the table all cleaned up and sat down.

"Yeah, what kind of changes would you make, Jack?" Joe repeated in a sarcastic tone.

Lisa handed out beers and gave Johnny a Coke. We popped the tops and all took a big swig.

It was hot and I could have used some water. I had to carefully word any advice that I would provide to Rico. I could tell he had taken some type of drugs because he looked high.

"Alright here's what I think, but you won't like it. First of all you don't need a daily meeting with everyone in attendance. Appoint or vote in a head person for each group. People you can trust to do the job. They can report to you daily and if they do their job well reward them. Make them your friends and loyal soldiers. They're your eyes and ears."

"That sounds reasonable to me," Lisa commented.

Rico countered, "Ok. I agree that sounds like a good idea. What else do you think?"

I took a drink of beer and a long drag on my smoke thinking how to proceed. I looked at Lisa who probably doesn't even know anything about the Constitution or how it came about. US history hasn't been taught in schools for years.

"I would have a security team of four men with me at all times. You're not making any friends here. On Tocabaga I have my family with me most of the time. We just had a revolt, a few days ago, and had to kill thirteen people, so make sure you know who you can trust. Don't think you can intimidate and bully people to get your way. You rule here by fear alone and some day that could bite you in the ass."

"Ruling by fear has worked well. That's the way all great rulers were successful. Keep the people hungry and make them live in fear," Rico stated.

Joe repeated, "Yeah, rule by fear works."

I gave Joe a disgusted look and said, "Rico, your thinking is so antiquated. Don't you remember a little document called the Constitution? You took an oath to support and defend it. Now you're violating it in many ways."

"Don't tell me about the Constitution. Look what our government did. Now there is no Constitution."

"Rico, you got it all wrong. We still have the Constitution but the government has tried to take it from us. We can't let that happen. We must honor and remember the Bill of Rights even if the powers to-be don't want us to. It's men like you and me that have to fight to keep our rights."

I looked at Johnny and saw he was enjoying the Coke. Johnny probably knew more about the Bill of Rights than Lisa.

Looking at Lisa I asked, "Do you know the

Bill of Rights?"

"The Bill of what?"

"The Bill of Rights."

She thought for a minute while twirling her short brown hair around her finger and replied, "Gosh, I don't know what you're talking about."

"See Rico, that's what I'm trying to tell you. We have to drum it into the young people what our country was at one time. Johnny, tell Lisa the first two amendments to the Bill of Rights."

"I don't know the exact wording. The First Amendment is freedom of speech. The Second Amendment is the right of the people to keep and bear arms."

Lisa responded, "Don't we do that, Rico?"

"Yeah Honey, we kind of do that."

"I carry a gun and I can say what I want."

"See Jack, it's hard to explain the difference. She wouldn't understand."

I commented, "You have to teach our whole history and the Constitution."

"I'm not running a school here," Rico advised.

Joe butted in, "He's not so smart, BOSS."

"Shut up, Joe, he's smarter than anyone else here."

I shook my head and told him, "You need to have one or two teachers who can spend the time to explain our history to the young people.

"Look it's getting late and Johnny needs his sleep. Where do we sleep tonight?" Johnny was dozing off.

"You can sleep in my room and I'll sleep with Rico tonight. I'll take you up to my room," Lisa suggested.

"Thanks for your input, Jack," Rico replied. Joe didn't say a word. I didn't trust Joe after his comments. I think he wants to be BIG BOSS. I could tell Joe the Hammer was resentful of my friendship with Rico.

Johnny was fast asleep so I picked him up in my arms carrying him to the room. Lisa opened the door revealing she had a real bed room set with a double bed. Lisa lit a candle as I placed Johnny in her bed. The windows were open which showed a view of the garden. A slight breeze was blowing in which helped to cool the room and remove any unwanted odors.

Lisa whispered in my ear, "Good night, Jack. If you need anything let me know. We're right next door. Feel free to use the shower." She planted a warm wet kiss on my cheek as she squeezed my arm. She smelled good, really good which made me somewhat intoxicated.

"Good night and thanks for letting us use your room." As she closed the door she blew me a kiss. How sweet she looked, but I knew she was really a deadly killer. Tomorrow we would see how deadly.

I laid down next to Johnny and thought we have to get out of here tomorrow one way or another. I knew my people were looking for us and it was just a matter of time before they came here. That could cause a serious situation to evolve.

JULY 3, 2025

I woke Johnny up at 6 am and we went for a short jog around the garden together. After that we each took a shower. I was just getting dressed when there was a knock at the door. Going to the door shirtless I opened it to see Lisa and Rico standing there.

"Hey, let's get some breakfast guys," Rico suggested.

"Ok, I'm hungry," Johnny replied.

Lisa eyed me as I put my shirt on. It was one of those eat em up looks. Rico and Johnny were already heading down the hallway toward the stairs. Lisa grabbed my arm and said, "Come on old man."

I hurried to tuck in my shirt, stuck the Glock in my waist band, and picked up the M4. Lisa commented, "You don't need all that fire power to eat breakfast."

"I know, but I don't go anywhere without my guns."

Arriving at the cafeteria we got in the chow line. The three new cooks were there passing out food. They had done a bang up job making western omelets and fried chicken.

Rico and Johnny were carrying on a conversation about the Constitution which surprised me. I could tell Rico was bonding with Johnny and it was doing him good.

I commented to Lisa while we were eating, "Tomorrow is the Fourth of July. Do you know what that means?"

"It's Independence Day."

"Right, but who did our country gain independence from?"

Johnny raised his hand saying, "I know, it was Great Britain." We all laughed because Johnny enjoyed the challenge of answering questions.

With breakfast done Rico said, "Let's go to the gym and work out."

"Great, let's go, Mr. Rico," Johnny blurted out. I chuckled at Johnny's enthusiasm.

Rico grabbed Johnny by the hand and they started to run to the gym. Lisa and I slowly followed them. She commented, "Johnny is good for Rico. I can see a soft side to him that I never saw before."

"Yeah Rico has a soft spot for kids. I'm surprised he didn't kill the pervert himself. Why did Rico even let Hank in the clan?"

"Hank was one of the first people in the clan and at the time we didn't know he was a pervert. When Rico found out he told him if he touched any kids he'd be dead meat. He never did so Rico just let him work in the garden by himself. He didn't have friends."

Arriving at the gym the free weights were set up over in a corner. I noticed that Joe was already here doing bench presses. Rico was showing Johnny how to warm up. We all started doing calisthenics following Rico's lead. Rico made it look easy putting us through the workout which consisted of 4x20 sit-ups, 4x15 pushups, 2x100 jumping jacks, and general stretching.

I looked at Lisa and her beautiful body was glistening from the sweat. I wasn't the only one watching her. Joe was eyeing her up and down like a hungry wolf. Joe looked at me and asked, "Hey old man how much can you bench?"

"I don't know, maybe two fifty."

"I'll bet ... you can't do two fifty," Joe commented as he grunted the weight up in the air.

"I don't need to bench that much weight."

I picked up a couple of twenty five pound dumbbells and started to do curls. Johnny was standing next to me doing two pounders. Rico had forty pounds in each hand.

"Why not?" Joe asked.

"I work out just to stay in shape not to build big muscles. I stay just strong enough."

"You can never be too strong. You're a wussy."

I ignored his comment but it was clear he had a thing for Lisa. Joe, wanted Lisa and maybe he even had thoughts about over-throwing Rico.

I finished my workout and told Johnny, "Let's go for another run." While the others worked out Johnny and I left the compound. On the way out I told the guards, at the front door, we'd be back soon.

We ran to the bridge on 54th Avenue that crossed Interstate 275. Johnny and I reached the bridge and stopped running. I thought this is a chance to escape and head back to Tocabaga. I looked at little Johnny and decided that it was too risky to walk all the way back to Tocabaga. There was no telling what type of bandits we could run into on the way home. I couldn't take the risk.

Standing on the bridge I looked north and south down Route 275. The road was empty except for a few abandoned vehicles on the side of the road. I sat down and contemplated what my next move would be.

Johnny said, "Let's go home, Grandpa. I know the way. We just go straight down this road." I laughed out loud because it was like he knew what I was thinking.

"It's not that easy, Johnny. There could be a lot of bad men between here and home. We'll have to go back to the compound and maybe we can leave tonight or tomorrow for sure." As we started to walk back I heard cars coming.

Johnny and I looked in all directions and then he yelled, "There're cars coming from the north." I looked thru my rifle scope and saw five trucks about half a mile away.

"Grandpa, it's Dad and Uncle Ron!" The kid has good eyes. He was right, it was my family and others from Tocabaga. We stood up on the bridge and waved our hands as they approached.

The convoy sped up the entrance ramp to 54th Avenue and stopped on the bridge in front of us. Johnny ran over to Tommy and gave him a big hug. Everyone jumped out of the trucks and they all asked the same questions. "Where have you been? Are you ok? How did you escape?"

I raised my hands to shush the group and replied, "We're fine. We've been here with the 54th Avenue Gang. I need to talk fast so listen up."

Tommy, Ron, and Jim Bo, along with my other trust-worthy warriors, gathered around me.

"I'll tell you later how we escaped. Y'all need to get back to Tocabaga right away. Stan told me the Feds were planning an attack to over-throw Tocabaga. The group of twenty people we let in the other day has some undercover agents. Any single men in the group throw them off the island as they are probably agents. Anyone who Albert doesn't recognize should also be removed.

"I'm staying here as a guest of Rico Martin. He's in charge of this group. It's called the Dimachaerus Clan."

Tommy commented, "Rico Martin, how's he doing?"

"He is meaner and crazier than ever. The Feds kidnapped his wife and son. He doesn't know where they're at and it has really affected his brain. He's gone to the dark side."

"When and how will you get back?"

"Take Johnny back with you. I need to stay here tonight to talk with Rico some more. Give me a phone to stay in touch. Rico will give me a ride back to the island. If he doesn't give me a ride then I'll call you to extract me.

"When you get back to Tocabaga put security on full alert."

We shook hands and I stood there watching them speed away. I was torn between going with them and staying here a little longer to help Rico find his way. I didn't wanna let down an old friend who needed my help. I slowly walked back to the compound thinking what could I say or do to bring Rico back into the real world. Maybe nothing could help him, but I had to try.

I arrived back at Rico's compound and it was 11 am. Rico, Lisa, and Joe were in the gym and as I walked in Rico said, "Where the hell you been? Where's Johnny at?"

"Well, we went for a run down to Route 275. We were just sitting there talking when we heard some cars coming down the road. I couldn't believe my eyes, it was my family. It was my son and brother with about twenty other people from my security team. They were driving around searching for us.

"Johnny went home with his Dad and I chose to stay here tonight like I promised I would. They headed back to the island."

"Damn, you should have brought them here to meet me. It's been a long time since I saw Ron and Tommy."

"Yeah, I know, but they needed to get back to Tocabaga to take care of some urgent matters. We're facing a possible Federal attack. I think it'll be tomorrow on the Fourth of July."

"In that case we'll get you back there after the fights tonight. You gonna need any help fighting the Feds?"

I thought about this for a minute and didn't reply right away. It would create a number of problems. I didn't want Rico on Tocabaga even if he was my friend.

"I don't think we'll need any help, but thanks anyway."

"Ok it's up to you. Let's get some lunch and then relax until the fights at seven pm. We'll warm up around six."

"I'm gonna miss Johnny. He's a great kid," Lisa mentioned.

"I agree," Rico stated.

Joe walked ahead of us to the lunch room.

He always stayed close to Rico when I was around. I could tell he wanted to know what we were talking about. I touched Rico's arm to slow him down.

I whispered, "Watch out for Joe. I think he wants to be King."

"No, not Joe, he's my body guard."

"I'm telling you he's got eyes for Lisa and the way he looks at you means trouble. I've seen that look of envy before."

"I'm not worried about it. Who doesn't look at Lisa? I saw you gawking at her during the work out. If you stay tonight you can sleep with her. I don't mind. She's a hot little thing and besides she likes you a lot."

"Thanks, Rico, but I don't operate that way. You know that."

"You're always so noble and honest. That's the one thing I like about you, but it's a weakness if you ask me."

I wanted to get Rico back on track and make him realize that Joe could pose a real danger to him.

Joe turned around and inquired, "Hey, you guys talking about me?"

Rico responded, "Yeah, we're talking about you. So what?"

"Be careful what you say about me, Jack. I'd hate to hurt Rico's only friend."

"Is that a threat, Joe?" I asked.

"Take it anyway you like, old man."

I nudged Rico's arm and he advised Joe, "If you have a fight with Jack then you have a fight with me. You got that, Joe?" Joe didn't answer back and walked away at a fast pace.

Lisa asked, "What the hell is going on?"

"Too much testosterone and roid rage. I don't think Joe and I are good buddies," I told her.

I sat down for lunch with Rico and Lisa. Joe didn't sit with us. The whole time he glared at me, from across the room, so I knew trouble was brewing. Joe sat there talking to some of the security guards and kept pointing in my direction. Joe was planning something with his henchmen. Rico seemed not to notice and I didn't point it out.

After lunch we went to our rooms to rest before the fight. Lisa went with Rico and I was staying in Lisa's room. I had just laid down on the bed and there was a knock on the door.

"Come in," I yelled with my gun in hand.

The door slowly opened and Lisa walked in. "Hi, I need to take a shower and clean up."

"Do you want me to leave?"

"No, it's ok, I'm sure you've seen a naked woman before." She dropped her halter top, pushed off her shorts, and wiggled out of her panties. Wow she was gorgeous.

As I turned my head the other way she commented, "Don't be shy. What do you think?"

I eyeballed her as she turned around showing me every profile of her naked body. She was posing in front of me displaying everything. Lisa was proud of her body and not ashamed to reveal it.

Scanning her up and down I whispered, "You're a ten for sure. Your body is perfect. Now go take a cold shower."

"Come and join me. I can tell you need a cold shower."

"I can't do that."

"Why? Rico don't mind at all. He sent me here, but I wanted to come anyway. I like you a lot, Jack." She stood there kind of dancing around in the nude.

"Lisa, I'm a married man."

"I don't mind and I won't tell her. You know I'm an exhibitionist. I like showing off, dancing in the nude turns me on. The more you watch me, the more turned on I get.

"That's how I met Rico. I was forced into dancing at seventeen to make money after my parents and brother were killed by the Federal Police. I grew to like it because it made me money. One day Rico came in and just whisked me away and I've been with him ever since."

"Come on Lisa go take a shower before I spank you."

"Ok, now you're talking!" She bent over right in front of me, sticking her bare ass out for a spanking.

Shit, I said the wrong thing. I couldn't help it; I had to touch that sweet looking butt. I gave her a little smack on the ass and said, "There you go, now take that shower."

She sat down on the bed next to me, started to rub up her hands over my chest, and asked, "Take me with you to Tocabaga when you leave. I'm tired of the fighting. I don't want to die fighting for Rico. I only do it to please him. That's how he gets his rocks off."

I didn't know how to reply or what to say. I was shocked by her comment.

"Please take me with you. I'll do whatever you want. I don't want to fight anymore. I don't want to fight tonight. Let's leave now while Rico is asleep."

"Has Rico ever hit you?"

"If I don't do what he says then I get hurt." She was afraid to tell me how abusive Rico has been. I didn't think this would happen.

"Lisa, let me think about it while you take a shower." She went into the shower room and I thought this situation has turned into a big FUBAR. If Rico's girl friend comes with me, he'll surely try to kill me and if he doesn't then Joe would try.

I heard the shower turn on so I phoned Tommy, "Did you check the list of people and throw the new single men off the island?"

"Yeah, everything went fine, but I found something interesting. There's a woman here named Maria Martin with her twenty year old son named Rico."

"That has to be Rico's wife and kid."

"That's what I thought, so I asked her if her husband was a Navy Seal. She said yes, a long time ago. She told me a story how the Feds kidnapped them."

"Ok, I'll tell Rico she's there. Don't tell her where Rico is. Here's what I want you to do … get four trucks and come to the 54th Avenue Bridge at nine tonight. I'll meet you there. Call me when you arrive. Be sure to bring plenty of fire power."

I hung up the phone and Lisa came out of the shower room with a towel wrapped around her. The thin white towel just barely covered her little butt cheeks.

Just then … KRASH … the door was bashed in. Standing in the doorway was Joe holding his big sledge hammer. He yelled, "What the hell's going on here?" Standing behind him were two other men.

"Get out of here you big jerk," Lisa shouted.

With that he ripped off her towel and ordered, "Put some clothes on you little slut," as he rudely pushed her aside to the ground.

Joe glared at me and then leaped towards me raising his hammer high in the air. I ducked as he swung the hammer at my head and reached for my Glock. He grunted as the swing missed my head. He raised his arm up again to strike me and I pulled the trigger … BAM … BAM … BAM. Three rounds hit him in the chest.

The hammer still came down and I raised my arm to block the blow while trying to move out of the way. The hammer dropped from his hand and we collided forcing me to the floor with him on top.

I saw the other two men enter the room with guns at the ready. Lisa screamed, "You bastards!" She seized her knife and jumped naked at one of the men stabbing him in the chest and face. She moved so fast it surprised me.

I saw the other one point his gun at her and I quickly aimed at his head, while laying on the floor, and squeezed off a round. BAM … the bullet hit him in head and blood splattered on the wall. I pushed Joe off me, stood up, and shot the Hammer in the head just to make sure he was dead.

Lisa had sliced the one dork to pieces. He looked like he ran into a buzz saw. She had pierced his heart with the sharp blade. Lisa stood there nude in a puddle of blood. Blood was splashed on her face and body. She started to shake and fell into my arms weeping. The fight was over.

Rico and four guards came running into the room. "What the fuck is going on?" Rico surveyed the room and saw his body guard was dead.

Lisa wrapped the towel around herself as Rico put his arm around her and inquired, "You ok, baby?" She nodded her head.

Rico looked at me, "You ok, Jack?"

"Yeah, I'm ok."

"What the hell happened?"

"Joe and these two dopes tried to kill me and Lisa. She took care of one and I shot Joe and the other guy. We had no choice. I think Joe had planned to kill me. He broke into the room and was surprised to see Lisa here. She came over to take a shower. He didn't count on her being here."

Rico stood there speechless, examining the bodies for a few minutes, and then said, "Joe was pretty stupid to try and kill you with his hammer." Then he started to laugh and told his guards to remove the bodies and clean up the blood.

Lisa went to take another shower as Rico and I walked outside the room. He handed me a smoke and said, "Let's get a beer buddy."

Sitting in the gym Rico popped open two beers and we chugged them down. "Jack, you tried to warn me. You were right about Joe. I think his plan was to kill you and then kill me. He wanted to run this clan and have Lisa to himself."

"You're right. That was his plan. We can discuss this later. I have something important to tell you, Rico."

"What's that?"

"Right before Joe broke into the room I was on the phone with Tommy. This is going to be a shock, but he told me that … your wife and son are safe on Tocabaga."

"How's that possible?" Rico looked at me in shock.

"A group of twenty people came to Tocabaga for sanctuary the other day. I didn't see your wife because the Marshals' kidnapped me. Tommy reviewed the list of people and found Maria Martin and Rico, Junior had signed the list. She confirmed that her husband was a Navy Seal."

"Does she know I'm alive and here? How do they look? How did they get free?"

"Ok, take it easy big guy. They don't know you're alive or here. Tommy didn't tell them yet. They're doing fine and are safe with us on the island. It's a long story, but they were being held at the Dome. The Rangers raided the Dome and set all the prisoners free a few days ago. Any how, they ended up coming to Tocagaba."

"There really must be a God. Thank you, God!" Rico yelled. He jumped up and hugged me a little too hard because I felt my back crack.

"Thank you, Jack. I owe you big time."

"You don't owe me anything. I'm as happy as you are."

"What do I do now? I can't let them see me like this. I haven't seen them for three years. I had given up all hope of ever seeing them again.

"Does Lisa know about this?"

"No, I didn't tell her anything."

"That's good. Don't tell her. I'll tell her when the time is right."

We sat there in silence. Neither of us spoke as he was thinking what to do. I was thinking what I could do. What if I was in his shoes? Granted it was hard to imagine being in his shoes. Just then Lisa came walking into the gym. She sat down next to us and noticed Rico had a concerned look on his face.

"Hey, what's up? Why the gloom and doom look?" Lisa questioned.

Rico snapped, "Not now, Lisa. I'm thinking about something."

"Maybe I can help." She rubbed his arm and gave him a little hug.

Rico pushed her aside and stated, "Don't bug me."

I said, "Lisa let's go for a walk."

We walked outside to the garden. All I could think about was that Lisa wants to leave the clan and come to Tocabaga. Rico's head is mixed up enough. I wondered what he was going to do if I told him.

Lisa picked a flower and handed it to me,

asking, "What's a matter with Rico?"

"He'll tell us when he's done thinking about it. I know he's concerned about replacing Joe."

"I never liked or trusted Joe. He was a dirty scumbag. I'm glad he's dead. I think Rico should pick Billy to replace Joe. He's polite and loyal to Rico. He does whatever Rico wants. Billy is strong and has a lot of energy. With some training he'd be a good fighter. He's a great shot and can handle any weapon."

"Well, recommend him to Rico."

"Yeah I will, but there is something else bothering Rico. Did you tell him I wanted to leave with you?"

"I swear, I didn't say a word about that. You need to tell him, not me."

"I'm afraid to tell him. I thought we'd just sneak away."

"No, Lisa, I'm not going to sneak away. You need to tell Rico the truth. I'll be there with you."

"The truth is I don't wanna die or get cut up. I'm also tired of his abuse."

"So that's what you tell him when the time is right."

I couldn't help but wonder when the time would be right. Right now he's thinking what to do about his wife and son. In a few hours the fights would start and he'll be all hyped up. The best time to tell him anything is when he's relaxed and mellowed out.

My thoughts traveled back in time. I thought back to the times Rico and I, along with a few other bad ass characters, would hang around together. They were all dead now except for Rico and me.

TWENTY YEARS AGO

As I explained earlier Rico and I met at the gun range. We became friends by shooting together every Thursday. He had just been promoted to SWAT Team Captain of the Tampa Police Department.

I introduced Robbie, Serious Chris, and, Crazy John to Rico. Rico began to bring his friend Stavros to the range. Soon we were all good buddies and would go out on Friday nights together.

Robbie, my best friend, was killed a short time ago on Tocabaga fighting the Feds. He was shot with a 50 caliber round blowing out his chest. He died on the spot with no pain. Maggie, his widow, is a Captain for my Amazon Warriors.

Serious Chris got his nick name from Robbie. Chris is serious about everything. He worries about everything, but is afraid of nothing. He spent twenty plus years training in the martial arts. He was fast and strong standing six foot and a 180 pounds. Chris got killed in a car accident, but we never thought it was an accident.

Crazy John was just an overweight wild guy who would do anything to make a buck. He hated to be called a chicken. If you called him a chicken those were fighting words. John didn't care who he got in a fight with. He never backed down and was pretty much fearless. That's why we called him crazy. In the beginning John wasn't a good fighter. He lost most of his fights but he never backed down from one. After three years of hand-to-hand combat training John became a lean, mean, fighting machine.

John never carried a gun which I thought was stupid. He always claimed he didn't need one. It caught up to him one day as he was coming out of a strip bar. He got into a fist fight over a stripper and the other man pulled a gun. Crazy John died on the spot. The Police ruled it was a justified self-defense shooting.

Stavros was really weird. He was a friend of Rico's and an ex-DEA undercover agent. He helped bust the Mob in Miami who were the main drug dealers. Stavros got caught taking a car as a gift from the Mob. He had to take it or they would have been suspicious of him. If they give you a gift you take it or else it's an insult. He was fired as a DEA agent and then got a job repairing guns in Tampa.

Stavros was an expert in hand-to-hand combat and in gun fighting. He always carried two Ivory-gripped stainless steel Colt 45s. On the grips' there was a Scorpion, which was his birth sign. He claimed the Mob had a hit out on him. Stavros was no one to mess with; he was six-foot-three and pushed 230 pounds. He had a fifty-four-inch chest with large gorilla-like arms.

Stavros did a lot of meditation and was into Oriental beliefs. The first time we had fight club we all went to his apartment. It was a small run down place located in a bad section of town. I remember the first time walking into his small one bedroom apartment. There wasn't any furniture, chairs, tables, TV, or bed. For lights he used candles.

He had three mannequins dressed in combat gear. He had stacks of meals ready to eat or MREs'. Stavros had all kinds of military supplies stored in every corner. There was a safe bolted to the floor which contained his weapons and ammo. That was how he lived.

Stavros ended up getting sick. He claimed it was lead poisoning from doing reloading and shooting. Anyhow he became sicker and never got better. The last time I saw him he could barely walk and I assume he died somewhere on the streets or in a jail. Maybe the Mob found him and bumped him off. I never found out what happened to him.

The six of us would go to local strip clubs, which we frequented quite often, and all the girls would come over to our tables. We were big tippers and the ladies liked that since they only work for tips.

We always carried guns, knives, brass knuckles, and other weapons everywhere we went. The six of us looked like gangsters since we each wore a dark blue sports coat to conceal our weapons. No one dared to mess with us, not even the real gangsters, because we knew most of them. Yeah, we had a few problems with the strip club Good Fellows, but when Rico showed his badge they'd all back down. If they didn't we'd kill em' in self-defense. We never killed anyone who didn't deserve it. You had to be a real bad guy for us to bump you off.

I recall one time Robbie went to a strip bar by himself which he did quite often. It was a bar that we never patronized. The Good Fellows working there put a Mickey in his drink and they followed Robbie as he staggered outside. They mugged him and took all his money. They beat him up pretty good so we decided to pay them a visit. Our plan was to bash some heads and break some bones.

They didn't know who we were but they knew Robbie. Robbie went in by himself and ordered a shot with a beer. They would bring the beer in a bottle and open it at the table. Robbie would drink the beer and then spit the shot into the empty beer bottle. The plan was after three drinks he would stumble outside, pretending to be drunk, where we would be waiting under cover.

We put on our brass knuckles when Robbie came out with three jerks right behind him. One dork grabbed Robbie and another punched him. Robbie had his knuckles on and punched the dork hard in the face as we came out from hiding. It was six against three and we had on the brass knuckles. Rico took great pleasure in breaking their arms. After we beat the shit out of them Robbie took all their money and then pissed on their faces.

After that we went inside for a drink and a lap dance. Someone saw the dorks laying in the parking lot and called the cops. An ambulance came and took them to the hospital. The cops came in the bar and asked us if anyone had seen a fight outside. Police Officer Manning, who knew Rico, looked at us and shook his head as he walked away.

We had our own little gang that was one for

all and all for one. Anyway we started fight club training every Sunday morning at a local gym. One gym owner let us use the space for free just to stay on our good side since we were all members. We would practice hand-to-hand combat, knife fighting, gun retention, and general fighting methods.

Rico was the Boss of all this. He was the cement or glue that held it together. I was his go-to man. When he wanted something done he'd ask me to follow up to make sure it got completed. I did a lot of dirty jobs for Rico. Jobs he couldn't do because he was a cop. He still owes me.

Rico ended up getting married and that pretty much ended our fight club gangster days after five years. We all moved on in our own directions. Robbie and I were the only ones that stayed close friends because we lived near each other.

"Jack! Jack, are you ok?" Lisa's voice brought me back from the Time Warp.

"Yeah, I'm ok. I was just thinking about the past."

"About the past?"

"Yeah, Rico and I go back twenty years and we had some good times in the old days."

"Fight time is coming up I have to get ready or Rico will be mad."

"I'll fight for you tonight. I don't wanna see you get hurt. One cut to your face could destroy those pretty looks."

We started to walk back to the gym. On the way I told her, "Don't say anything to Rico about leaving until after the fights."

Arriving at the gym Rico waved us over to him. He was sitting in his throne and as we approached he stepped down. Putting his arms around us both Rico said, "I love you both. You're my real friends. You're the only ones I can trust."

I found his comments very un-Rico like.

"Tonight I'll fight both men. I'll fight Ken first and then Allen. I need you both to be my back up. After what happened with Joe I don't trust anyone. I need to show these idiots that I'm in control.

"After the fight I want to discuss something with both of you. I want to discuss our future."

It was almost fight time. The people were slowly coming in the gym and taking a seat along the side lines. The torches' were lit as the sun was setting. Rico sat back down on his throne with Lisa to his right. He signaled me to sit on his left. Four armed guards were standing to my left side.

Rico handed me Joe's hammer and commanded, "Start the games, Jack. Bang the hammer."

Taking the hammer I stepped down to the floor ... BANG ... BANG ... BANG.

I yelled, "The BIG BOSS will now speak." The crowd hushed and all paid attention.

I couldn't believe that Rico suckered me into being his number two man.

Rico shouted out, "Joe and two of his guards are dead. They tried to kill Lisa and Jack. Let that be a lesson to everyone. All traitors will be killed on the spot.

"Let the fights begin! Bring in the Marshal and Allen Jones. I'll fight the Marshal first." The guards dragged in the two victims. Ken and Jones had no idea what they were in for.

Lisa stood up and stated, "Here are the rules. There are two white circles painted on the floor. Fighters must stay within the twenty foot outer circle. If you go outside the circle intentionally you lose the fight. Knives will be placed inside the two foot inner circle.

"You'll stand on the edge of the outer circle. When the whistle blows run and pick up one or both knives. This is a fight to the death. There is no surrender. There is no quarter given. Prisoners, do you understand the rules?"

Neither one replied. I wondered if they were prepared to die.

"No reply means you understand the rules," Lisa yelled.

Lisa handed me Rico's Black Bear and her knife. "Jack please place the knives in the center ring."

Two guards had to force Ken up to the outer circle. He stood there looking at me and cried out, "This is murder! I don't know how to knife fight. I'm a nobody. I won't say anything to anyone."

No one said a word as Rico walked down to the circle. Lisa was putting the whistle to her lips when Ken suddenly ran to the inner circle. He picked up both knives before Lisa blew the whistle. Rico stood there and chuckled. Lisa finally blew the whistle.

Ken screamed, "Ok BOSS man come and get me!"

The guards were going to shoot Ken, but Rico stopped them and commented, "He's all mine."

Ken stood in the center of the twenty foot

circle with both knives, swinging them back and forth, trying to scare Rico. The crowd roared as Rico stepped forward into the ring of death. The gym was filled with people all cheering and screaming, "Kill the Fed." It was being chanted over and over.

Rico stopped, raised his big muscular arms, and flexed his muscles. He flexed his pecs and the crowd cheered louder. Step by step Rico moved forward. I knew what he was going to do because I had fought him many times. The fact that Ken had both weapons didn't faze him at all. Lisa and I sat there carefully watching the action evolve.

Ken stood his ground even as Rico closed within a few feet. He was wildly swinging the sharp blades back and forth in the air. Ken was slashing at the air daring Rico to attack him. He bellowed, "Come on! Come on! Come and get it!"

Rico answered, "I'm going to enjoy killing you! Prepare to meet your maker!"

With that the crowd went crazy. Everyone cheered, "Kill him BOSS! Kill him BOSS!" They were a blood thirsty group of thugs. Even the women, who seemed to be drunk, were enjoying the suspense.

Suddenly someone threw a beer can at Ken hitting him in the back. Ken turned his head, just for a second, and that was a big mistake. In a flash Rico grabbed both his wrists. Ken couldn't move either arm as Rico twisted his hands in towards his body. Ken was going to stab himself to death with the help of Rico.

Ken dropped the blades from his hands and they bounced on the floor. BOSS let go of Ken's left arm and took hold of his right arm with both his hands. BOSS twisted Ken's arm so the elbow was showing. He had him in an arm lock. Rico put all his strength on the elbow and bent the arm back until you heard it pop. Even over all the noise you could hear the arm snap.

Rico stepped back and took a deep breath. He stood there looking at Ken who was holding his broken right arm screaming in pain. I was thinking now is the time Rico will kill him. I knew it was going to be painful.

Ken put up very little resistance as BOSS picked him up in the air over his head. The crowd went wild as Rico went down on one knee and dropped Ken back first onto his other knee. CRACK ... his back snapped and Rico tossed him to the floor like a rag doll.

I could hear Ken moaning, but he wasn't moving. BOSS man picked up his Cold Steel blade and moved on top of Ken. I knew Rico was going to make him suffer more. BOSS jumped on Ken's back with both feet and you could hear Ken moan as the air got knocked out of his body.

BOSS raised the Black Bear as he grabbed Ken's hair pulling his head back. Rico slit his throat about half way thru, but not enough to cut the jugular veins. Blood poured from his neck and gurgled out of his mouth as he slowly died drowning in his own blood.

Rico stood up and the crowd cheered. Women threw him flowers. People were screaming, "Long live the BIG BOSS!"

Rico turned and looked at me for approval. I nodded my head a little but I wasn't smiling or yelling. I looked at Lisa and she didn't look happy either. This was what Rico lived for. He loved the attention and the killing.

While they dragged away the body Rico walked over to the cooler and popped open a beer which he chugged down in one gulp and said, "Bring the next one for slaughter."

Allen Jones watched what Rico did to Ken so I'm sure he was trying to figure a way out of this. Allen looked like a tough guy who could handle himself. Maybe he would fair better.

I picked up the knives and placed them in the center ring. Lisa stood up and stated, "Fighters make ready on the circle."

The men took up their positions on the edge of the ring. Unlike Ken, Allen showed no fear. They stood there glaring at each other. It was a tense moment waiting for Lisa to blow the whistle. Both men were crouched down ready to make a dash for the blades. Suddenly she blew the whistle and they sprinted for the blades.

Allen was pretty fast and reached the knives the same time as Rico. The BOSS didn't bend down to pick up a knife. As Allen bent down to grab one Rico kicked him in the face knocking him backwards to the ground.

As Allen flew backwards BOSS picked up his Cold Steel blade but didn't go after the invader. He waited for him to get on his feet. Rico flexed his muscles again and growled for the crowd. Everyone yelled, "Kill the invader!"

As if on cue a bunch of people tossed beer cans at the invader. He ducked them and moved around the circle but didn't approach the BOSS man. People started to boo and threw more stuff at him. Rico stood there just watching Allen move around the ring.

They were about fifteen feet apart when Allen took the knife by the blade and threw it at Rico. Rico tried to dodge it but the razor sharp blade stuck in the right side of his chest. Rico stood there looking at it and then pulled it from his chest muscle. He tossed the blade outside the ring as blood ran down his chest.

It was clear Allen knew something about knives since he knew how to throw one fast enough to hit a target like the BOSS man.

Rico growled out, "Now I have to hurt you boy! I'll cut you too pieces!"

Once again the crowd chanted in unison, "Cut him to pieces!"

BOSS man moved forward with his knife in the standard fighting position. Allen removed his shirt and wrapped it around his left hand and forearm. This told me he knew what he was doing. Wrapping a shirt around your arm is a good way to stop a sharp blade from cutting you.

As Rico approached him Allen took off his belt, which had a large buckle, and began to swing it around in the air at a super fast speed. WHAM ... the buckle hit Rico in the hand knocking the Black Bear to the ground. Rico jumped back as the buckle just missed his head. The blade was on the floor in between the two men.

The swinging belt buckle kept pushing Rico back. He was at the edge of the white line. If he crossed it then he would lose the fight which meant death. The crowd gasped and Lisa shouted, "Rico, get him now!"

BIG BOSS put his head down and charged like a bull, hitting Allen in the gut, taking him to the ground. Somehow Allen managed to flip Rico over. It surprised me that Allen was so strong and wiry. They laid on the floor with the knife within their reach. Both men stopped and stared at the blade. Suddenly they jumped for it at the same time. Rico had the strength and skill but Allen was no push over.

I knew when fighting a strong guy like Rico you needed to use his strength against him. You need to know one or all of the following fighting styles such as Judo, Jujutsu, Hapkido, or Aikido.

Allen knew how to use Rico's strength against him. I was getting worried that this nobody could beat the great BOSS man. Allen however made a big ass mistake while grappling for the knife. Rico managed to put him into an arm bar.

I could see Rico pull on the arm as hard as he could. You could see Allen was in pain. He was yelling as BOSS kept pulling on the arm trying to break it. Then all of a sudden Rico let go and pushed Allen aside. Rico picked up his knife and stood there for a second looking at Allen lying on the ground writhing in pain.

Rico walked around the ring flexing his arms and the people cheered him on. As BOSS walked around the ring Allen stood up with his right arm dangling at his side completely useless. He just stood there watching Rico walk over to him. The two men were standing about four feet apart and the crowd hushed. Rico lowered the Black Bear and put it in his scabbard. You could hear a pin drop.

Rico looked at Allen and said, "You gave me a good fight. Where'd you learn how to fight?"

Allen replied, "I was in the 101st Airborne for twenty years. I used all my skill, but you're too strong. I figured you were a Navy Seal when I saw the Trident tattoo on your arm."

"I spotted the Screaming Eagle tattoo on your shoulder and that's why I stopped fighting."

Someone yelled, "Kill the invader!"

Rico held his hands up to hush the mob and shouted, "This man is a fellow warrior! He served in the Army and therefore he's free to leave! The fight is over, so everyone clear the room."

As the people filed out of the gym Rico took Allen to the cooler for a beer. Lisa and I walked over and sat down with them. Lisa had some antiseptic and some super glue to seal the one inch wound in Rico's chest. I looked at it and determined it wasn't that deep or serious. Rico acted like it was nothing at all.

Rico asked Allen, "How's your arm?"

"It hurts like hell but I'll be fine in a few weeks. It's not broke just some pulled ligaments and tendons."

"Good. I'm glad to hear that. This is Lisa and Jack Gunn."

We shook hands and I said, "You should have told us you were in the Army."

"I didn't know if that would be good or bad. There are so many crazy gangs around you never know. Some of them not only kill Federal Police but anyone who's been in the military."

Lisa inquired, "How come you hooked up with the 38th Avenue gang?"

"I was passing through, walking down Route 275, and they approached me in a friendly manner. They offered me some food and a place to sleep. They're good people for the most part. I think you can trust them, but I've only been with them for a couple of weeks."

"Yeah maybe we could make an alliance with them. Who runs that group?" Rico asked.

"For the most part there is no one man in charge. They are disorganized and need some military structure. They have a group of six people who call all the shots. They're called the Council.

"I like the way you run things here since it's

more or less like the military. You give orders and people follow them. Their system nothing gets done because no one can make the final decision. Everything is done by consensus of agreement."

Rico commented, "If you like it here why don't you stay and become my number two man and head of security."

"You want me to be the number two man? Who's number one?"

"Lisa is number one."

Allen asked, "What about you Jack? How do you fit into the group?"

"It's a long story, but I'm just visiting. I'm leaving tonight." I looked at my watch, it was 8 pm.

Rico told Lisa, "Take Allen to the clinic and get him some pain killers and an ace bandage for his arm. Set him up in a room for the night and then come back here. I need to talk to you and Jack.

"Allen I'm sorry for the mix up. I never like to hurt a fellow warrior. Get a good night's sleep. I'll see you tomorrow and explain what your new job will be."

"Ok, BOSS see you tomorrow."

As Lisa and Allen left the room, Rico advised me, "Jack, I've been thinking what to do about my wife. I love her and my son, but I also love Lisa. I'm a different man than three years ago. I need to change and not be such a control freak.

"I don't want to hurt Lisa but I want my wife and son back. If they come here it would never work out with Lisa here. It would confuse my feelings. Every time I see her I want her. I'm asking you to take Lisa with you to live on Tocabaga."

Wow, that just made things a lot easier. Now Lisa can leave the clan and become an Amazon Warrior.

"Of course Lisa can come with me. I promise you she'll be happy on Tocabaga. I'll make her an Amazon Warrior. That's my all-women police force. So she'll have a job and her own place to live."

"That sounds great, Jack."

"I think with Allen here and your family you can make big improvements. Get rid of fight night. It's turning everyone into a blood thirsty mob. That would be my first step. Have your wife teach school to the kids here. Try to make things as normal as possible. Get rid of any bad eggs living here."

"Yeah, you're right. I need to make things as normal as possible. You're going to come back once a week to help me out. Right?"

"Of course I will. When Lisa comes back I

suggest you tell her right away she can to leave with me."

"No, I can't tell her. You ask her to go with you."

"Ok I'll ask her. I didn't tell you this, but Tommy is coming here at 9 p.m. to pick me up. I'm meeting him at the bridge on Route 275."

"Great, then tomorrow can you bring my family here?"

"Yeah, I'll bring them here by noon. Here comes Lisa now."

Lisa advised, "Ok, Allen is all set up. Now what do you want to talk about, Rico?"

Rico hung his head looking at the ground. He needed me to speak up for him. He couldn't summon the words to tell Lisa to leave.

I spoke up, "Lisa, how would you like to come to Tocabaga and live?"

Lisa looked at Rico afraid to speak. Rico still didn't look up. She asked him, "Rico, would you let me go with Jack?" Rico nodded his head yes. Lisa asked, "Really you don't mind?"

"Yes I mind, but Jack just told me that my family is on Tocabaga and I need them here with me. I love you, but it wouldn't work out if you're here along with my wife and son."

"Yeah, sure Rico, you're right it wouldn't work. I think you should be with your family. It's better that way for sure."

My phone rang, it was Tommy. "We're here at the bridge."

"Ok I'll be there in about thirty minutes.

"Our ride is here, Lisa. Collect what you need and let's get going."

"I got a bunch of stuff. It'll take me an hour to pack."

"Come on we'll help you pack." We went to her room and filled up one large suit case and three Army duffle bags. The three of us carried her gear down to the waiting trucks.

Rico shook hands with Tommy and Ron as we loaded her bags. Tommy asked, "Who is this?"

"Hi, I'm Lisa a friend of Jack's."

"She's coming to Tocabaga to live with us," I stated.

Tommy looked at her and I knew what he was thinking. I punched him lightly in the arm and said, "Let's get going."

Lisa gave Rico a big kiss and I yelled, "I'll be back by noon tomorrow with your wife." We pulled away with Rico standing there broken hearted.

Riding back to Tocabaga Maggie was in the truck with Lisa. They looked at each other in a curious way and I introduced them.

I commented, "Maggie, would you take Lisa under your wing and get her settled on Tocabaga?"

"Sure Jack, no problem."

Lisa said, "It's great to meet you. I love your Army outfit. Are you in the Army?"

"No I'm an Amazon Warrior. There are twenty of us on the island and we're an all-woman Police force."

"Wow, that's cool."

I butted in, "Lisa knows how to fight, and has a lot of experience using guns. I think she'd make a great Amazon."

"Good, we have an opening."

"Ok, show her the ropes and discuss it with Amy and Trini."

Maggie looked at her, "You can stay with me. I have two spare bedrooms. Each one has its own bath. We can be roommates until we find you a place to live."

"That's really nice of you. Thank you," Lisa responded.

By the time we arrived on Tocabaga it was late. I walked into the house and Hemmi was sitting there waiting for me. I sat down next to her and told her the whole story. I was dead tried and just wanted to have a shot of JD and go to sleep.

JULY 4, 2025

I woke up feeling pretty good. I could hear the birds singing outside my window. It's Fourth of July, one of my favorite days. It was 7 a.m. so I went down stairs for some breakfast. My whole family was already up.

As I walked into the room, everyone yelled, "Happy Fourth! Welcome home!" I hugged everyone and responded, "It's good to be home."

Tommy asked, "Ok tell us what happen. How did you escape from the Marshals?"

"Didn't Hemmi or Johnny tell you?"

"No they didn't. We asked but they told us to ask Grandpa."

"Well, the truck ran out of gas. Then a gang

came along and captured us. They took us to meet their leader, BIG BOSS, who lucky for us turned out to be Rico. That's what happened in a nut shell."

"Who's the hot chick?"

"Her name is Lisa. She was Rico's girl friend and wanted to come to Tocabaga. She's one tough cookie. Rico trained her how to fight. Amy needs to make her an Amazon." Amy nodded her head in agreement.

"Today we need to reunite Rico with his wife and son. Tommy, advise Maria and her son we found Rico and to get ready to move out ASAP. We should leave early before the dirtbags are up and roaming around the streets looking for food. I promised Rico we'd be there by noon."

Late in the afternoon derelicts start roaming around looking for food, guns, or anything they can steal. I call these people Free Roamers. They aren't part of a large clan or gang. They're usually small groups of people consisting of three to ten people. These are tough, dangerous people who will kill you without a second thought. It's the Wild West all over again. Kill or be killed is the motto one needs to go by. Shoot first ask questions later is what I always say. The Free Roamers pick on the weak and helpless. They live on the streets and die on the streets.

Tommy asked, "How many trucks should we bring?"

"Bring two Hummers, the SUV and one pickup truck. We'll need two men in each vehicle. Be sure the lead Hummer has an American Flag flying from the antenna," I advised.

We usually have the lead truck fly the Stars and Stripes from the antenna. That makes people stop and think twice before shooting at us because they assume it's a military truck.

It was 10 a.m. and the trucks were lined up at the bridge ready to leave. Maria Martin walked up to me with her son. She gave me a hug and a kiss on the cheek. "Jack, it's great to see you again."

"It's good to see you, Maria. You look really good."

"This is my son Rico, Junior." He held out his hand, which I shook, and said, "It's a pleasure to me you. We're taking you to meet your Dad. He's waiting for us at his compound on 54th Avenue."

Little Rico was not so little. Standing around six feet tall at an estimated 160 pounds, he was a fine looking young man.

Maria asked, "Why doesn't he come here to live?"

"He has his own compound and soldiers.

Don't worry. You'll be safe there. Ok if everyone is ready let's go."

Tommy inquired, "What route do you want to take."

"Let's take I-275 there and come back on Route 19."

It's always a good idea not to retrace a route because the Feds or gangs could be waiting your return and ambush the convoy on the way back.

We pulled out across the Tocabaga Bridge with Tommy and Tony in the first Humvee. I was driving the black Fed SUV with Ron riding shot gun. Maria and Rico, Jr. sat in the back.

Rico said, "I can't wait to see my Dad. Is he doing ok?"

"He's doing fine. I just spent two days with him," I answered back.

We drove by the destroyed condos which where shelled by the Rangers in three major battles. One battle was with a large gang, one with the Federal Police and another with al-Qaida. All of them tried to take over our island. The ruins included the old Eckerd College. It was a shame to see these once wonderful structures sitting there with exposed beams, no roofs and broken windows. Large holes were blown in the walls of every building by the Iron Maiden's 120 mm cannon.

The Iron Maiden is an Abrams Tank based at Tocabaga for security. The M1 Abrams Tank, named after General Abrams, fires a whopping 120mm laser-aimed cannon and never misses its target. The cannon can blow up buildings. It has one M2 50 Caliber Heavy Machine Gun, and two 7.62 M240 machine guns. Bullets and other large projectiles just bounce off the sides of this big boy.

As we approached the Dome we could see a Federal road block, on the Interstate, about a half mile away. We stopped to discuss the situation.

"It looks like four trucks and about ten men. What you wanna do?" Tommy asked me.

"I wonder what they're doing."

Ron suggested, "Let's get off the interstate and take Route Nineteen to 54th. There's no sense in taking any risks."

I agreed so we took the 22nd Avenue exit ramp. As we sped down the exit ramp we were surprised to find two more Federal trucks blocking the road. They spotted us and we didn't have time to turn around. Tony started to fire his fifty caliber M2 machine gun.

Tommy shouted over the radio, "Pedal to the metal!"

All our vehicles skirted around the Fed trucks and we fired at them as we drove past in a speedy fashion. The agents were surprised by our convoy and didn't have any time to return fire.

Jim Bo, driving the last Hummer, radioed, "They're coming after us!" Chris, his gunner, turned the machine gun and started to pepper the vehicles with big fifty rounds. Since their trucks were more or less normal pickups, with no armor, they stopped after a few rounds pierced the front of their vehicles, bringing them to a stop.

"They stopped chasing us," Jim Bo radioed.

Tommy, in the lead truck kept the speed up at fifty miles per hour. We saw a few people every now and then walking around the streets but no one shot at us. Most waved as we passed by and we waved back, but a few gave us the finger.

Every now and then we saw a beat up car sitting on the side of the road. We passed a few slow moving vehicles. They didn't pose any danger to us. Since red lights haven't worked in years we didn't stop for anything. No one stops for them anyway. If you stop you're a sitting target for some sniper or a car jacker.

We arrived at the 54th Avenue with no

further incidents. We crossed the bridge which goes over Interstate 275. I radioed Tommy to stop on the east side of the bridge. I didn't want the convoy to pull up near Rico's compound for fear of being shot at by mistake.

Maria, little Rico, and I dismounted and walked about a hundred yards to the old school. The guards yelled, "Hey Jack, what's up!"

"Tell Rico, his wife and son are here!" We waited outside the main door and in a few minutes Rico appeared in the door way. He had on a clean shirt and I noticed he shaved his head getting rid of the Mohawk. He looked half way normal.

He just stood there, in a daze, checking out his family. Maria ran to him and they hugged each other. Little Rico shook his Father's hand. All of them started to weep. I stood back giving them room. After a few minutes Rico looked over at me and smiled.

Rico wiped the tears from his eyes as he approached me. I looked at the ground and kicked a rock making it seem like I didn't notice his tears. He said, "Jack, you're the best friend I have. Thanks for bringing us back together."

"No problem. We gotta go, but I'll be back next week. Take this phone so we can stay in touch. You need anything let me know." We gave each other a high five and I jogged back to the truck.

My men were standing in the street waiting for me and I told them, "Mission accomplished. Let's go home and party. It's Fourth of July!"

As we mounted up, Tommy asked, "Which way back?"

I replied, "Let's take nineteen back home."

Ron reminded us, "We'll need to be on the lookout for the FPF on the way back. They could be hanging around 22nd Avenue waiting for us."

"You're right. By the way what do we have in the way of weapons other than the big machine guns?"

"We have our M4's, two SAWS, one MK153 with two reloads, and five hand grenades," Tommy advised.

We were just getting ready to leave when my phone rang. It was Captain Sessions. "Hello Jack, I'm calling you to advise we're delayed and won't be back to Camp Tocabaga for another two days. I wanted to warn you about the new warlord in your area. His name is BOKO KANG, also called THE DRAGON."

"I read an Intel report about him. What else can you tell me?"

"These guys are the worst. They're radicals

who take no prisoners except for teenage kids. Male kids become converts and soldiers. Females are forced to work for the soldiers doing whatever they want them to. They get them hooked on meth and then dope them up before they go into battle. KANG gets his nick name, THE DRAGON, because he uses flame throwers to burn everything, including people."

"Captain, he sounds just like the kind of dirtbag I'd like to terminate."

"His body guards are all young kids and they are dangerous. His troops consist of about two hundred grown men and one hundred young kids."

"Ok Captain, thanks for the warning. Stay safe out there."

"I'll email you Kang's picture to your Tocabaga.Jack gmail account. See y'all later."

I advised my men on the arrival of the DRAGON into our area. All we can do is hope they don't come to Tocabaga. I fear sooner or later we'll have a run in with the warlord BOKO KANG.

I define a warlord as a leader of a ragtag military group who fights against other leaders, groups, or governments for territory and/or monetary reasons. The warlord usually maintains control of his men by the use of violence or bribes. Because of this the entire group was prone to being a band of blood thirsty cut throats.

As we were mounting up I commented to my men, "Maybe that's why the Federal Police were on Route 275. They were looking for the DRAGON."

"Yeah, they're probably worried about what that group could do to the Green Zone," Jim Bo stated.

"I just wanna get back to the island and get our defenses ready in case they show up."

We drove to Route 19 and headed south toward home. Off in the distance we could see black smoke billowing into the sky a few miles away. We stopped to observe it.

"Maybe one of the Fed trucks Chris shot caught on fire," Tommy suggested.

I responded, "Yeah, it's probably the tires burning. Let's keep going and find out."

When we reached 22nd Avenue South we found the two Federal Police trucks that chased us earlier. They were burning in the middle of the street along with four bodies that were charred into a black jell. The burnt bodies were a disgusting smelly sight. The legs and arms had been hacked off their bodies.

Ron commented, "It looks like the DRAGON has been here."

We started scanning around the area. I told Tommy, "Drive west down 22nd Avenue for a few miles and see if you can spot anyone." In the meantime Ron went east looking for the KANG boys. Everyone else was keeping a sharp look out with guns at the ready.

Tommy radioed, "I found them. They're at the old Twin Brooks golf course. I only see three trucks with about twenty men. Maybe there are more of them but I can't tell from here."

I replied, "Ok, get the hell out of there before they spot you. Let's get back to the island."

We arrived back on Tocabaga with no further problems. I called a security meeting to put our personnel on full alert. I filled everyone in on what we were up against which was some of the most dangerous scumbags on the planet.

We had already set Claymore mines along the Tocabaga entrance road. They were mounted in the metal guard rails along the road and were painted to match the rails. We called this the Road of Death because if these mines were exploded anyone driving or walking down the road would be killed.

We had our full security team of ninety six men plus twenty Amazon Warriors on full alert. It was decided to cancel any Fourth of July celebration. We would celebrate when the Rangers returned in a few days.

I held a meeting with my key people to discuss the possibility of taking some kind of offensive action. Tommy suggested we should try and assassinate BOKO KANG and his Generals. He suggested we send a sniper team tonight making a preemptive strike. The logic was if we cut off the head of the DRAGON then the little Dragons may fade away. With no one to lead them the group would fall apart.

This made a lot of sense to me so I asked Tommy, "How many men do you need?"

"I'll need one man for spotting and one to be our rear guard."

"I'll be your spotter so we need a volunteer to be our rear guard. Before anyone steps forward think about it because this is gonna be dangerous."

Brogan stepped forward, "Count me in."

Brogan has been here since the beginning. Everyone likes Brogan he is a friendly person who would help anyone out. Before the collapse he ran a car parts store. He knows every part on most cars.

Brogan trained hard to be a member of the security team. He takes his security job very seriously and is an excellent shot. He has good reflexes and is light on his feet and fast. Brogan is pretty much fearless and he won't crack in the heat of combat. He's not a big guy, but he's tough as nails.

No one knows Brogan's first name. Everyone just calls him Brogan. I was pleased he stepped forward because 1 knew we could count on him. He was perfect for the sniper work we had to do.

Tommy advised, "Great. We got our team. We'll leave as soon as it gets dark. We need two Humvees to drop us off at the old National Guard Armory on 37th Street. Each truck will have a driver and gunner. They'll wait there for our return or radio call to be picked up. Tony and Ron will be in one Hummer and Jim Bo and Chris in the other.

"I'll recon the perimeter of the golf course first looking for the best location to set up our snipers' nest. I'll have my .308 with a silencer, but all our weapons should have sound suppression."

"How close are we going to get to them?"

Brogan asked.

"I don't know, but we need to get within six hundred yards," Tommy replied.

I butted in, "The main objective is to kill KANG and if possible a few other bastards. Then we leave and do it the next day. My plan is to keep them wondering who is going to get killed next. Then maybe they'll move on or disperse."

"What about the kid soldiers? Will we shoot them?" Tony asked.

"Yeah the kid soldiers are a big problem. If they shoot at us we have no choice but to terminate them. If they surrender we'll take them in. If they run away we let them go."

Tommy said, "Here's the plan. We'll go north on 37th Street to the Armory. I want to leave here at 2100 hours. Since there's no moon tonight it'll be pitch black by the time we hump to the golf course. Maintain radio silence unless it's urgent. If there aren't any more questions then we meet at the bridge at 2100 hours."

It was 1700 hours so we had some time to get our gear ready. Since this was Brogan's first sniper hunt I pulled him aside and advised him to duct tape all his gear down so nothing rattles. I told him to bring three hundred rounds of ammo and to put some camo paint on his face and hands.

Three hundred rounds of ammunition means you need to carry ten thirty round magazines. Each mag is about one pound, so you have to carrying ten pounds of ammo. Then you have water, a bullet proof vest, tactical vest, boots, and your gun. So you have to be in pretty good shape to run around with about fifty pounds of gear hanging on your body.

It was 2100 hours and everyone was at the bridge. Tommy checked out Brogan and me for loose gear and rattles. Then I checked him out. He ran through a check list making sure we had all our gear and supplies. The three of us huddled together and I said, "God give us the strength and courage to complete this mission. Protect us from evil. Amen." We all bumped knuckles and jumped into the Humvee.

The Humvees dropped us off at the Armory which was now just a burned out shell of a building. They parked off the street, across from each other, hidden in the over-grown bushes.

As my sniper team dismounted Tommy commented, "I'm taking point and Brogan you're the rear guard. Just watch what's behind us. We don't want anyone sneaking up on us. Keep spaced out about twenty feet apart. If I duck you duck. If I hide you hide. If you see anyone behind us shoot first and ask questions later."

Brogan replied, "Ok, I got it."

"Brogan, can you see anything without those glasses?" I inquired.

"Yeah, I can read, but distance is a big problem."

"Do you have a spare pair?"

"Are you kidding? I'm lucky to have these." I nodded my head in agreement.

We proceeded down Thirty Seventh Street and we didn't see any anyone alive. We only saw burned up bodies lying around in the street and dirt. As we approached the golf course perimeter we heard a lot of noise. It sounded like the dummies were having a party.

Tommy crawled forward, for a look see, while Brogan and I laid waiting in the high grass for his return. Tommy was doing a recon to pick out a good sniper location. We had a lot of cover because the grass and weeds were waist high. There was no shortage of over grown bushes or trees. We blended in with the bushes hiding in the grass waiting for Tommy to return.

I hate going though high grass or weeds because of snakes and spiders. Believe me we have a lot of those, but the biggest problem is a little plant named a Sandspur. This is a type of grass that grows in sandy soil in the warm south. One blade of grass has hundreds of sharp prickly burs which carry the seeds. The Spur or bur is about the size of a pencil eraser. These burs have little hooks on them and stick to any type of surface. They get all over your clothes, shoes, and skin. These little burs hurt like hell and feel like little needles. They are almost impossible to remove. If you try to brush them off the hooks break off in your skin and cause an infection. The best way to remove them is to put saliva on your fingers and pull them off one at a time.

We had Sandspurs all over us because we couldn't see them in the dark. We heard music, people singing, and drums beating. I didn't like all the noise because it was difficult to hear what was around us. The good point was they couldn't hear us either.

I heard a voice so I peeked over the edge of the tall grass and saw two men or boys walking in our direction. It was too dark to tell how old they were but they were coming our way. They were about fifty feet away from death. I racked a round into my M4 and whispered to Brogan, "Two bad guys coming this way. Stay down."

I could hear their voices but couldn't see them due to the high grass. They seemed to be coming closer. Now they were standing very close to me. I guessed they were just a few feet away. They stopped walking and stood there neither one speaking.

Then one said, "Did you hear that?"

The other replied, "It's just a bird or animal."

All of a sudden one man fell on top of me and then the other. It scared the shit out of me. I fired three bursts at them as they tumbled to the ground next to my feet.

I didn't hear the shots that killed them. Blood flowed from their heads. The bullets went in the back of their heads and made a big exit hole blowing off most of their faces.

I heard another person coming through the grass and stood up holding the M4 to my shoulder ready to fire. I saw it was Tommy so I lowered my weapon.

"I saved your butts," Tommy whispered as he appeared out of the grass.

"I had them in my sites," I replied.

Tommy laughed, "Yeah sure."

Brogan helped me drag the bodies, rolling them under a bush, and we covered them up with some big palm leaves.

"I found a spot that we can shoot from and it provides us a good escape route. The DRAGON and his henchmen are at the club house. The driving range faces it. We'll be about four hundred yards away at the end of the driving range. There aren't any trees in the line of fire," Tommy advised.

Tommy bent down and drew a map in the dirt of the whole layout.

"There's a clump of trees here. This is where we'll shoot from," he commented.

He drew another line in the dirt saying, "This is a stream or river that runs by the golf course. We need to cross it here to gain access to the trees for cover," as he pointed his stick.

"The plan is to kill KANG and as many of his men as we can. We'll keep shooting until they discover our location and then we'll withdraw the way we came in. Any questions."

"Are there any more of their guards around?" Brogan asked.

"I didn't see any but keep alert."

"Let's get going and get it over with," I told them.

Tommy replied, "Ok we're going to take the old Skyway Trail to the point where we need to cross the river. Once we get to the water watch out for gators."

"Shit, I hate gators. What do we do if we see one?" Brogan asked.

"Shoot it in the back of the head if it comes after you."

We reached the little stream and started to cross. It was deeper than we thought. The water was waist deep so we lifted our guns up high to keep them dry. Recent rain had flooded this little stream turning it into a river flowing at about three knots. The footing was tricky because of slippery stones on the bottom.

I was about half way across the twenty foot wide river when I heard a splash behind me. I turned around and saw Brogan's head come up from under the water. He stood there looking in the water.

I asked him, "What the hell you doing? This isn't a time to go swimming."

"I lost my glasses."

I softly replied, "Come on, you're not going to find them." I kept wading towards shore but Brogan was still looking for his glasses. Tommy was on shore and moving into a sniper position among the trees. The noise from the DRAGON party was getting louder.

"Come on Brogan, your glasses are gone man." He kept looking as I climbed up the slippery bank out of the river. I laid down next to Tommy and we started scoping out the targets.

Tommy asked, "What the hell is he doing?"

"He's looking for his glasses."

I turned around to look at Brogan, who was a good forty feet away, and he was diving under the water.

"The hell with his glasses, he could get us all killed," Tommy replied.

Tommy and I laid there scoping out targets. I estimated there were about two hundred men camped in the area. They had fires going and were in little groups of five to ten men. I counted ten trucks and four cars.

Then we saw the DRAGON. There was no mistake it was him sitting on the club house patio smoking a cigar. He was a fat guy with a black beard and wore a yellow turban around his head. All his men wore a yellow bandanna around their necks or on their heads.

Tommy advised, "Get ready, I'm taking him out."

I watched through my rifle night scope as Tommy took careful aim and pulled the trigger …

POP … and in a split-second the bullet hit KANG in the chest. He slumped to the ground while the men around him seemed unsure what was wrong with their Boss. A couple of men ran over to him. They didn't hear the shot. Tommy shot again and again killing two more men before they all ran for cover inside the building.

There was no movement around the club house. We waited for a few minutes and then I saw a couple of guys running towards the building. I told Tommy, "Targets at ten o'clock."

"I got em'." He fired two more rounds taking both men out. They dropped dead right at the front door. "UPS delivery," Tommy said, while laughing.

Looking to the far left I saw two trucks headed in our direction. They were loaded with men and I could see muzzle flashes. Then we heard the bullets whiz overhead. We ducked and Tommy advised, "Time to leave."

We turned around and crawled down the bank into the water. I shouted, "Brogan, we're out of here!" I scanned around, looking in all directions, but there was no Brogan.

We quickly waded across the water and climbed out just as the trucks arrived. A group of men lined the bank. They were firing everything they had in our direction as we jumped behind a couple of trees. I don't think they saw us because none of the bullets were hitting our trees.

I peeked around the tree and saw them shooting into the water. We crawled away in the darkness and finally reached the Skyway trail. We stopped out of breath and I asked, "What the hell happened to Brogan?"

We heard the men splashing across the river still shooting their rifles. Tommy replied, "We can't do anything about Brogan. I just hope he got away. We'll come back and look for him tomorrow. We gotta go right now!"

We could hear the bushes moving and men yelling. The bad guys were closing in on us. We took off in a dead run down the trail. Tommy would get ahead of me by a hundred feet and then stop to cover my back. I would run a hundred feet past him and I would stop to cover his retreat. We alternated this way all the way back to the waiting trucks firing as necessary.

The DRAGON men were hot on our heels. As we approached the trucks Tony asked, "Where's Brogan?"

We jumped in the Humvees and I replied, "Brogan just disappeared. We don't know where he is, or what happened to him." Tony is Brogan's best friend and I could tell he was worried and upset that Brogan was not with us.

"How the hell did that happen?"

"Brogan lost his glasses in the water and the last time I saw him he was swimming around looking for them. When we started shooting the bad guys I thought he was right behind us acting as our rear guard. The DRAGON men started to come after us so we had to withdraw but Brogan disappeared. We didn't have any time to search for him."

Tony started the motor and he yelled, "Here they come!"

As we pulled away both Hummers opened up with the M2 fifties, blasting away at the crowd of twenty or so men running down the street wildly firing their AK47s. I saw many fall, maybe dead or just falling, to avoid the deadly stream of fire from our machine guns.

Soon we were out of range and out of their sight. I told Tony, "We'll go back at first light and look for Brogan."

Tony replied, "Count me in on the search."

We arrived back on Tocabaga with no further incidents. Tony dropped us off at my house.

We all agreed to meet at 9 a.m. to search for our friend. Tommy and I had a drink and hit the hay. I couldn't sleep thinking about Brogan. What the hell happened to him?

JULY 5, 2025

It was seven a.m. and we were standing at the bridge. We had to make a plan fast to go find Brogan. I wanted some additional fire power and suggested that we bring two SAWs along just in case, four additional men, and one more truck.

My men all agreed so ten of us loaded up our gear and mounted up. Soon we arrived at the Armory and we spotted eight bodies in the street but they weren't alone.

Three big gators were also in the street devouring the dead bodies along with wild dogs and vultures picking up the scraps. We observed the gators ripping the bodies apart, tearing off large chunks of meat. The dogs would quickly dart in and out grabbing a piece of meat, while staying away from the gators. There wasn't much left of the corpses.

"I wonder if those gators ate Brogan?" Tony asked.

"Yeah, being eaten alive is a hell of a way to die," Ron stated.

I told everyone, "Ok stay alert. The gang could still be around. I want a team of four for the search party. Tommy takes the point. Jim Bo, Ron, and I will be in the middle. Tony you're the rear guard.

"Everyone else stay here and guard the trucks. Let's move out."

We gave a wide berth to the gators and proceeded down the Skyway trail to the river crossing. Tommy ran ahead of the group to see if the DRAGONS were still around. He reported back that the KANG boys were gone. They had pulled out of the golf course, so we moved forward with our search.

The river flowed south so we went south guessing if his body was in the water it would be washed in that direction. Two of us were on the east side and two on the west side of the river searching for Brogan.

Tony asked, "Where does this flow to?"

"It flows into the bay. There's a bunch of

mangroves at the mouth. It's only about a half mile away," I replied.

Mangroves are dense shrubs that grow in coastal swamp areas. They have big tangled roots that make passage almost impossible. If Brogan's body is in the tangled roots we'll never find it.

We reached the mangroves where the water is brackish. We didn't see any gators along this part of the river. There were no signs of his body so we decided to backtrack and go north. It took us another hour hiking though the dense grass and weeds. It was hot and progress was slow. Every now and then one of us would yell out for Brogan.

Traveling north the water becomes almost clear and the mangroves disappear the further you are from the salt water. As we walked along the river bank we did see a few more gators. Tony shot a couple of them in the head for the fun of it. After going about a mile we decided to call it quits and go to the club house for a look see. Along the way we scouted around the golf course.

We spread out in a line with fifty feet between us and moved west to east toward the club house. By the looks of it these people cleared out pretty fast because some tools and junk where left behind.

We reached the club house and on the

ground we saw the bodies of the DRAGON and the four other men we shot. His yellow turban was missing.

There was a big fire pit that had some meat still burning in the hot coals. It smelled terrible and I held my breath as I walked by the black smoking meat.

I told Tommy, "Let's check out the house. I'll be right behind you." Tommy slowly opened the door and walked in with me right on his back. We scanned the big room and saw nothing but plates on the tables with food that had been half eaten. I proceeded to check out the locker rooms.

I could smell it, the smell of death, the smell of rotting flesh, as I walked into the shower room. Laying in the shower was a bloody torso of a body. It was just a torso, no head, no arms, and no legs. It had been chopped up or a better word would be butchered.

Tommy walked in and said, "Holy crap! Is that Brogan?"

"I don't know there's no way to tell who it was. Let's look around to see if we can find any evidence if it is Brogan." Everyone started to search inside and outside the building.

I told Tony what we found in the shower room and he ran in to look at the body. Tony came back out and told us, "That's not Brogan."

"How do you know?" asked Tommy.

"Brogan had an Eagle tattoo on his right shoulder blade. That's not him."

"Hey everyone look at these plates. These look like finger and hand bones. The DRAGONS must be cannibals," Tommy commented.

We all gathered around gawking at the bones. They were human fingers all right and some were toes. These people are really crazy. Actually no one knew what to say about the eaten human body parts. It was a disgusting sight that sent chills down my spine.

I told everyone, "Keep searching. If you find anything bring it to me."

I went outside to get away from the stink. I removed my hat and wiped the sweat from my face. I closed my eyes and saw an image of glasses in my brain. They were at the foot of a tree.

As I have said before I'm lucky at finding any thing that is lost. I get these visions in my head. I don't know where they come from, but a picture just appears in my brain when I close my eyes.

I opened my eyes and there was one tree close by. I searched around the tree in the high grass. There was a rope on the ground and a lot of blood-stained grass. I was just ready to give up when I saw a shiny glint of reflected light.

Bending down I pushed the grass aside and found a broken pair of glasses. I yelled, "Tony are these Brogan's glasses?" Tony ran over to look at them.

Taking them from my hand Tony studied them closely and replied, "Yep, I think these are Brogan's, but I'm not positive."

We all just stood there until Tommy advised, "If those are Brogan's then the DRAGON boys must have captured him. We gotta find out where they went and get Brogan back."

I stated, "Let's think about this. There are three things that could have happened to Brogan. He could have been killed by the gators. He could have been killed by the DRAGONS. He could have been captured by the DRAGONS. We searched all over and couldn't find him so we know he's not here."

"So we have no choice but to see if he is being held by the DRAGONS," Tony said.

Everyone gathered around looking at the glasses. We were thinking or trying to guess where did this band of killers disappear too?

Since Tommy is our best tracker I told him, "Go check 22nd Avenue for any clues as to which direction they headed." The rest of us waited for him to return and discussed the situation.

Tommy returned with good news. "They clearly headed west on 22nd because their trucks left mud tire tracks on the street. Judging by how dry the mud is I'd guess they left here about day break. That means they'll be looking for a place to camp for the night. Does anyone have any ideas?"

Jim Bo spoke up, "They could be anywhere, but if I was them I'd try to get as far away as possible."

I countered, "Good thinking. We know that 22nd Avenue goes to Pasadena so they could go south or north. South takes them to the beaches and towards Tocabaga. North takes them away from us."

Then it hit me they were going to Tocabaga. It was the only place that they could obtain what they wanted most which was guns and food.

I informed everyone, "Listen up, here's what I want to do. I'll take one Hummer and follow the KANG gang down 22nd Avenue. I'll advise their location when we find them. I want Tommy and Jim Bo to go with me. The rest of you head back to

Tocabaga and get ready for battle. If the DRAGON men come down the Road of Death let them have it. I don't care how old they are. Anyone who wants to kill and eat us is going to die."

My men concurred and we headed back to the vehicles waiting for us at the Armory. I decided to call Rico and warn him about the cannibals roaming around our area. Rico offered his help but I advised him to stay put and be on full alert. I informed him of my plan and the fact that they may be headed to Tocabaga.

Our men headed back to the island and we zoomed down 22nd Avenue after the gang. Along the way every now and then we saw a burning body or car. These bad guys would kill and burn anyone they saw.

We were going over the Pasadena Bridge to St. Pete Beach which gives a clear view for about a half mile down the road until the point where the road bends. Tommy, standing in the gun turret yelled, "Slow down and stop! There's a person walking in the street about five hundred yards ahead."

As he was looking through his binoculars Tommy commented, "The guy has a yellow bandanna around his neck and an AK. He's a Dragon boy."

I pulled off the road, near some bushes behind another car to stay out of sight. We sat there and visually searched the entire area looking for any more people. "Do you see anyone else?" I asked.

"Nope, no one else is around," Tommy told us.

"What do you think he's doing by himself?"

"He might be the rear guard. Why don't we capture him and find out what he knows."

"How are we going to do that? If he's the rear guard then the main force must be close by."

"I'll shoot him in the arms and legs with my 308. I'll just wound him. I still have my silencer on. Then we just drive up and question him."

Jim Bo stated, "Yeah let's do it." I nodded my head for Tommy to proceed.

Tommy dismounted and started creeping forward, keeping low using bushes for cover, to be closer to the target. He moved to within one hundred yards and laid on the ground to steady his aim.

Just as Tommy was taking aim the guy turned around and looked in our direction. Tommy had a perfect shot. POP ... the man dropped his AK47; he was hit in the shoulder. He was knocked to the ground by the force of the bullet. Tommy then shot one of his legs. He couldn't move and was ours for the taking.

The 168 grain Bob Tailed Hollow Point cartridge is a devastating round. At one hundred yards the velocity is 2,600 ft/sec. and it provides 2,670 lb/ ft of energy. It can kill an elephant with no problem.

I started the motor, picked up Tommy, and drove over to the KANG boy. We jumped out with Jim Bo standing guard as Tommy and I stepped up to him. He was laying on the ground withering in pain and was severely bleeding. My guess was we didn't have long to question him before he would bleed to death.

The DRAGON boy was about eighteen years old. His shoulder had a two inch hole in it and he was shot in one leg. The bullet must have hit his femoral artery because he was bleeding out.

He couldn't move and twisted his head up to look at us. He mumbled in pain, "Who are y'all? Why y'all shoot me?"

I questioned him, "Where's your gang?"

"Mister, please help me." He was getting weaker by the second. Tommy tied a tourniquet around his leg to stop the bleeding.

"Ok, we stopped the bleeding now tell us

where your gang is at?"

"They're at the hotel with the big tower. Give me some pain killer!"

"Tell us where your DRAGON gang is going next and we'll give you something."

"Man, I don't know. I'm just a soldier."

"Did you capture a man at the golf course?"

"Yeah, we found a guy."

"Where's he at?"

"I don't know where he is. I think he's dead. Who are you guys?"

"We're the men who killed BOKO KANG last night."

"You didn't kill the ... DRAGON. The DRAGON has many ... heads."

The kid slumped over. The life had drained out of him so Tommy released the tourniquet and his blood flowed on to the sidewalk.

Tommy asked, "What the hell did he mean the DRAGON has many heads?"

"Damn if I know. I do know that you killed KANG."

Tommy expressed, "Well we know where they are, but we still don't know about Brogan. It's not looking good. Hey, this guy has a radio. I'll bring it along maybe we can use it to monitor them."

"Grab his yellow bandanna maybe we can use it later."

The radio was a standard hand held model good for a six mile range at best. It was tuned to channel four.

I looked at my watch and told my men, "It's getting late so let's go. We'll back track the way we came so no one spots us." We mounted up and drove back to Tocabaga. We were tired and disappointed.

We arrived at our sanctuary with no further problems. It was almost dark as we went to the bar for a drink. Tony was there and questioned me, "Did you find Brogan?"

"Sorry we didn't find him. We don't even know if he's alive. We captured one of the DRAGON boys and he told us that Brogan was probably dead. Right now the gang is at the old Tower Hotel."

"Well ... let's go look for him. I can't stand not knowing what happened to him."

"It's late and we need rest. We can't do any more today. The KANG group might come here tomorrow so we better be ready. Right now we can't do anything to help Brogan even if he's alive."

We wound up the meeting and I went home to my wife and kids. I was too pooped to stay awake and fell into bed. The bed felt great, but as I laid there Brogan kept haunting me.

Tomorrow we might have a major battle with the DRAGON men, but I wasn't worried about that. We have defeated better gangs and even the Feds. What did that kid mean the DRAGON has many heads'?

It really bugged me that Brogan was Missing in Action. Even if we find him how would we rescue him? Maybe we could make a trade of some kind. Maybe we'll need to use force to free our friend.

I know one thing I'll never give up looking for Brogan and neither will my men.

That's all for now.

GOD BLESS AMERICA, LAND OF THE FREE, AND HOME OF THE BRAVE!

Jack Gunn

PS: Read my article below on Gun

Selection. It gives advice to first time gun buyers ... how to choose the correct gun for defense or hunting.

GUN SELECTION

This article will cover gun selection based on what is the most popular ammunition. The gun is your most important asset. Without ammunition, however, your gun is worthless. What kind of guns should one own? Based on my 40 years of gun experience the type of gun and caliber is very important for your protection. Guns have only two main purposes which are hunting and self protection. Of course, any of the guns mentioned in this article can be used for hunting as well as self defense. The question is which gun is the best tool for the job.

For people new to guns I try to explain the differences in a simple manner. When purchasing your first gun it is a confusing matter to choose the correct gun with the large selection in the market. I have had many people ask me, what type of gun should I purchase? Where do you go to learn to shoot?

GUNS FOR HUNTING

The most popular ammunition is the .22 long round and the 12 gauge shotgun round. This ammo is easy to obtain and that is what is important. The more popular the ammo is the easier it is to find when you run out of ammunition.

I break down guns into two categories which are hunting guns and tactical guns or combat weapons. There may come a time when you will need to hunt for food. There are two types of hunting guns that can dispatch most animals and that is a 12 gauge shotgun and a .22 caliber rifle or pistol. These two guns allow you good flexibility. The shotgun you can use bird shot for hunting birds or rabbits and slugs for hunting deer or larger animals. In addition a 12 gauge with slugs or buck shot is a great weapon to use for protection at close range.

The one drawback is that shotgun shells are expensive and heavy to carry and too large to store many of them. Shotguns come mostly in semi-automatic and pump type. They hold 5 to 8 rounds. The difference is the semi-auto you just load and pull the trigger. The faster you pull the trigger the faster it shoots. The pump needs to be pumped or cocked each time to shoot it. I prefer the semi-auto type because it is faster, easier to clean and use. Double barrel or single shot shotguns are not worth owning since you have to reload every time you fire it.

Do not under estimate the .22 rifle or long

barrel pistol as it can be used on birds and or small rodents as well as be a tool for self defense. A .22 with hollow point bullets is an easy weapon to use and you can carry a lot of ammunition since the bullets are so small. You can store 5,000 rounds of this ammo in a desk due to its small size. A .22 rifle has a 200 yard range and 6 inch barrel pistol has a 50 yard range.

The 12 gauge shotgun and a .22caliber rifle are a must to own. A .22 rifle also comes in pump or semi-auto types. The choice is up to you. As for 22 pistols there is only one that I will mention and that is the Ruger target model as it is the best you can buy.

My selection for a shotgun is a Remington semi-auto model that handles 2 ¾ inch shells. Purchase a shotgun that has a stock and forearm that is made of modern plastic as it can stand up better to the elements.

GUNS FOR SELF DEFENSE

There are many types of combat pistol and rifle ammunition. The selection of the ammunition is critical to the type of combat rifle or combat pistol you will select for protection. The shotgun and .22 rifle mentioned above are dual purpose weapons but are mainly for hunting. The pistols and rifles mentioned below are really the weapons you need for total protection. These are guns that contain high capacity magazines.

What other types of guns do you need to survive? Well let us first look at what is the most popular type of ammunition used to make our selection. Having enough ammo will be your biggest problem. The fact is most police and military handguns are 9 mm. The 45 caliber and 40 calibers are also popular but not as common as 9mm luger ammo. The 9mm ammo is also less expensive to purchase.

For rifles there are only three major types of calibers that are widely used by the police and military. One is the .223 Winchester also known as the 5.56mm NATO round. The other is the AK 47 round 7.62 x39, a round used by the military and some police around the world. This is the most popular ammo used by terrorists and gangs because the AK 47 is an inexpensive weapon or rifle. The last is the .308 Winchester round or 7.62x51 NATO.

The .223 ammo is used by the famous Colt AR15 or the M16 which is now named the M4 carbine, widely used by our military. There are many different manufactures of the so called AR15 design. Some of these AR designs also shoot 7.62x51 NATO which is the basically the same as the .308 Winchester and are called AR10 rifles.

The 7.62x39 and 7.62x51 are not to be confused as they are totally different rounds. The drawback of the 7.62x51round is the cost is higher than the .223 and when you are hauling around 300 rounds they are also heavier. The 7.62 x 51 is a long range round and can exceed 800 yards. The .223 round has an effective range of up to 500 yards.

You can also purchase an AR type rifle that will fire the AK 47 7.62x39mm round. Bushmaster is one of the best manufactures for AR type designs which can be purchased in many different calibers. Several companies also make a .22 caliber AR rifle such as Colt and the Smith and Wesson M&P 15-22.

The most popular type ammunition for a pistol is the 9mm luger round. The most common type for a rifle is the .223 Winchester, also known as the 5.56mmNATO round. Knowing this we can select a number of different pistols, rifles, or carbines to use. For this selection we need to keep in mind durability, ease of cleaning, interchangeability, and ease of use by men or women.

Knowing that we want a handgun that shoots 9mm luger rounds you can note that all 9mm are semi-auto design and are not revolvers. Semi-auto means it has a magazine that holds the bullets and some can hold up to 18 rounds before reloading. There are two handguns that I recommend which are a Glock and a Springfield Armory model XD. I own both and they are the best dependable handguns on the market. This is not to say there are not other good brands but based on my shooting experience buying one of these handguns you cannot go wrong.

My favorite is the Glock Model 17 because it is dependable and very easy to clean and repair. Yes, sometimes guns break so you should have some extra parts or a backup gun or two if possible. Each gun comes with an assembly manual and the Glock can be taken apart by just removing the slide and one pin which is pushed out. I have shot thousands of rounds and only had my Glock break one time. The trigger return spring broke and I replaced it in 10 minutes with a new one. It is so simple that anyone can work on it. The Glock can be dropped in the mud, run over by a truck and still shoot. It can be fired under water and the barrel life is 350,000 rounds which is more than you will ever shoot in your life time.

Basically all AR15 type rifles are the same design and are easy to take apart for cleaning. The models may have different names from different manufactures such as Armalite SPR Mod 1 which is basically the same as a Colt CAR15 or carbine model of the AR 15 rifle.

It pays to buy a good quality rifle from a well known manufacturer even if it may cost a little more. Remember your life may depend on this weapon. If you buy an AR type rifle then find out what parts you may need to replace by asking the manufacture. I recommend buying two weapons of the same type this way you have a back up and you do not have to learn about different weapons and the assemblies. Parts between different manufactures' are not necessarily interchangeable. The AR15 can be cleaned in about 10 minutes just by pushing out a pin which opens the rifle up. It is also light weight so men and women can use it. The recoil is very low which is important for accurate firing. I recommend the Colt brand AR15 .223 as this is a dependable weapon which has been on the market many years.

Some manufactures such as Colt have also made CAR15 carbines that use the pistol 9mm luger round. This is an excellent weapon that has very little recoil but has a limited range of about 100 yards. It is made for close quarter combat situations. Having a CAR15 9mm is a good choice since you can use the same ammo as your 9mm handgun.

To summarize the guns needed are; a 12

gauge shotgun semi-automatic type, a .22 rifle or target pistol, a 9mm luger Glock handgun, and a .223 (5.56 NATO) AR15 design rifle or a CAR15 9mm carbine. I would choose to have two guns of each type so you have a backup. How much ammo do you need? It is up to you to decide, but the more the better as the gun is worthless without ammunition. If you can only own one or two guns then the AR15 rifle and the 9mm Glock are my choices.

Everyone in your family should know how to shoot each type of gun. I suggest one gun for each family member. Gun selection should be made by what each member of the family likes best to shoot. One may like a .22 caliber and one may like a 9mm Glock. Remember your family is also your Army to help protect each other. So proper training is very important. Do not spare any expense on training. Do not buy cheap unreliable guns.

GUN SAFETY

If you have no experience with guns then it is suggested that you learn by going to your local gun store or shooting range and take lessons from a good instructor. If you have a friend who shoots go with him to the range. The National Rifle Association or NRA is a valuable resource to use for this learning process.

NRA has safety rules which you can find listed on line. The worst thing you can do is buy a gun and not know how to use it or even load it. If you are faced with a threat to your life or that of your family then you better know how to use the weapon with some degree of skill. The more skillful you are the better your chance of survival will be. We are talking life and death situations that require split second decisions on your part so shooting practice is a very necessary. Join a local shooting club.

I stress do not buy a gun just to have one. Do not buy a gun if you will never practice or shoot it. How much practice do you need? Based on my experience I think shooting your weapon at least one to two hours per week is necessary to become a good shot and learn to know everything about your gun. I know many people who shoot two hours a week. I also stress go take combat shooting lessons at a gun school such as Gun Sight or Front Sight. They will train you in Home Defense, Vehicle Defense, Tactical Rifle, Pistol, and Shotgun use. Be the best you can be as learning to shoot is more than just going to the range and pulling the trigger.

Above all be a safe shooter and follow the safety rules. When not in use keep you guns locked up so kids cannot access them and they cannot be stolen from you. I strongly suggest a gun safe to store your guns and ammo as it will give you peace of mind. You can also keep other valuables in the safe. Shooting can be a great hobby providing much enjoyment and fun for the whole family. Shoot safe and shoot straight.

DRAMATIS PERSONAE

Albert Madison – Navy Vet. that comes to Tocabaga with his wife and two kids

Allen – A twenty year Airborne Vet. who fights Rico

Barry – A quisling killed by the Gunn family

Billy – Kid found living on the street with his sister Rosie and brother Peter

Boko Kang – aka the Dragon is a feared warlord

Bok Lam – A Chinese man and close friend of Jack's since high school

Brogan – A Tocabaga security guard who went MIA while fighting the DRAGONS

Buck – Motorcycle gang leader killed by Maggie

Chase – A quisling

Colonel Turner – Commanding Officer of the Army Rangers based at Fort Desoto

Corporal Phillips – In charge of the communications office at Fort Desoto

Captain Sessions – Combat officer, commands and controls combat operations in the field

Captain Riley – Female tank commander, girl

friend of Captain Sessions

Chris – Tocabaga security guard and close friend of Jack

Dew – A quisling killed by the Gunn family

Dr. Carl Urban – The inventor of the RCCD Units and friend of Jack's

Dr. Carl Urban, Jr. – Son of Dr. Urban

Dr. Alvin Sinclair – Robot inventor and Commie killed by Jack

Ellen – A lonely woman

First Lt. Fisher – TALOS Warrior, Platoon commander

Farmer John – An old farmer saved by Jack, now living on Tocabaga

Guy Allen or **GA** – Suspected spy living on Tocabaga was killed by Jack

General Harper – Commander of the Rangers located at SOCOM

George Taylor – A nice kid who was bullied in school by Nick

Hank – A pervert killed by Jack Gunn

Hemmi – Wife of Jack Gunn

Joe the hammer – Second in command under Rico, killed by Jack

Joe – RCCD tech. Supervisor; a tough guy killed by Jack

Little Johnny – Adopted grandson of Jack's

Johnny the Fisherman – A quisling killed by security

Jill – A warrior killed by Feds

Jim Bo – Husband to Amy and son-in-law of Jack

Jimmy Smith – A bully from years ago

Ken – US Deputy Marshal who went missing

Leroy – The man who killed Jack's little brother Mike

Lisa – Rico's hot girl friend

Maria Martin – Rico's wife

Mike – Jack Gunn's little brother killed by a doper

Maggie – Wife of Robbie, who is in charge of the farming

Mr. Johnson or **Famer John** – Old time Farmer

Mr. Horn – Pig farmer and dirtbag who wanted to kidnap Maggie for breeding

Nick – A bully from Junior High School

Peter – Little nine year old brother to Rosie

Rico a.k.a. BIG BOSS – Long time friend of Jack Gunn

Rico, Jr. – Rico's son

Rosie – A fifteen year old girl Jack found living on the street

Robbie – Best friend of Jack Gunn, a Tocabaga security guard killed by the FPF on April 27, 2025

Ron – Brother of Jack Gunn Retired Navy vet. Part of Tocabaga security.

Rick – President of Tocabaga Association, security team member

Sally – A warrior killed by Feds

Scotty – A quisling killed by security

Sergeant Hammer – Army Ranger

Sergeant First Class Dale – killed in action

Sergeant Major Willis – Ranger squad leader and security guard for Jack

Sergeant Cain – the Drone Master

Sergeant Smith - Army Ranger assigned as security guard for Jack

Stan – Deputy Marshal

Sue – Wife of Albert Madison

Tommy Gunn – Son of Jack Gunn and a retired Marine Scout Sniper

Tony – Bar keeper and sharp-shooter for Tocabaga

security

Trini – Amazon Warrior who killed Troy

Troy – A quisling killed by security

Victor Elway – An old farmer from Ellenton now living on Tocabaga with his friend Farmer John

Zack – A quisling killed by the Gunn family

OTHER BOOKS BY THOMAS H. WARD

THE TOCABAGA CHRONICLES:

TOCABAGA 1: Revised Edition

TOCABAGA 2: Theoterrorism

TOCABAGA 3: Warm Blood – Cold Steel

TOCABAGA 4: The Talos Warriors

TOCABAGA 5: The Quislings & Androktones

TOCABAGA 6: The Dimachaerus Clan - Missing In Action

TOCABAGA 7: Pàn Guó Zuì - High Treason

TOCABAGA 8: The Invisibles

CONTACT THOMAS H. WARD:

Website: www.ThomasHWardBooks.com
Email: Tocabaga.Jack@gmail.com
Facebook: www.Facebook.com/Tocabaga

www.ingramcontent.com/pod-product-compliance
Lightning Source LLC
Chambersburg PA
CBHW051520170626
46811CB00002B/907